Fabulous Fathers

Lenore stared at her son. What would he come out with next?

"Come on now, Timmy. You can't honestly expect Paul to drop everything and take us all on vacation? Paul can't just take off at the drop of a hat." And thank heaven for that.

"I suppose I could take a week off. That would give us ten days," Paul offered.

Lenore was horrified. "You can't mean it."

Paul shrugged. "Why not?" And, in fact, why not? She was one fine-looking woman, and while he had no intention of remarrying, just lately he could see his way clear to a little cuddling by the fire.

"Please, Mom?" Lenore tried not to look at her son's face, knowing she'd cave, but her head turned of its own volition. "All right, all right, we'll do it."

Oh, drat. What had she gotten herself into? If the bears didn't get her, Paul probably would. And the worst part was, she was having trouble convincing herself that would be such a terrible fate.

Dear Reader,

This month we have a wonderful lineup of love stories for you, guaranteed to warm your heart on these chilly autumn nights.

Favorite author Terry Essig starts us off with love and laughter in this month's FABULOUS FATHERS title, *Daddy on Board*. Lenore Pettit knew her son, Tim, needed a father figure—but why did the boy choose her boss, Paul McDaniels? And how did Tim ever persuade her to let Paul take them all on a cross-country "family" vacation?

Those rugged men of the West always have a way of winning our hearts, as Lindsay Longford shows us in *The Cowboy and the Princess*. Yet, when devilishly handsome heartbreaker Hank Tyler meets Gillian Elliot, she seems to be the *only* woman alive immune to his charms! Or, is this clever "princess" just holding out to be Hank's bride?

Anne Peters winds up her FIRST COMES MARRIAGE trilogy with *Along Comes Baby*. When Ben Kertin finds Marcie Hillier, pregnant and penniless, he gallantly offers marriage. But Marcie longs for more than Ben's compassion—she wants to win his love.

Jayne Addison brings us a fun-filled Western romance in *Wild West Wife*. And don't miss Donna Clayton's *Fortune's Bride*—a surprise inheritance brings one woman unexpected love. And, in Laura Anthony's *Second Chance Family*, reunited lovers are given a new chance at happiness.

Happy Reading!

Anne Canadeo

Senior Editor

Please address questions and book requests to:
Silhouette Reader Service
U.S.: 3010 Walden Ave., P.O. Box 1325, Buffalo, NY 14269
Canadian: P.O. Box 609, Fort Erie, Ont. L2A 5X3

DADDY ON BOARD

Terry Essig

Silhouette
R O M A N C E™
Published by Silhouette Books
America's Publisher of Contemporary Romance

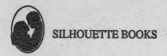 SILHOUETTE BOOKS

ISBN 0-373-19114-6

DADDY ON BOARD

Books by Terry Essig

Silhouette Romance

House Calls #552
The Wedding March #662
Fearless Father #725
Housemates #1015
Hardheaded Woman #1044
Daddy on Board #1114

Silhouette Special Edition

Father of the Brood #796

TERRY ESSIG

says that her writing is her escape valve from a life that leaves very little time for recreation or hobbies. With a husband and six young children, Terry works on her stories a little at a time, between seeing to her children's piano, sax and trombone lessons, their gymnastics, ice skating and swim team practices, and her own activities of leading a Brownie troop, participating in a car pool and attending organic chemistry classes. Her ideas, she says, come from her imagination and her life—neither one of which is lacking!

Fabulous Fathers

Dear Angie,

It's your birthday today. Seven years old. Weren't you just born yesterday? Your poor dad is getting old, kiddo. I know you can hardly wait to be a grown-up, but frankly, I wish you'd stop growing up so fast. I wish I was giving you this letter now instead of fifteen years from now when—if—I get up the courage to give you this notebook I've been keeping since you were born. And if you only remember one thing about your old man, remember this: I loved you. *I do!* And if I've made mistakes raising you, they were honest ones.

As a carpenter, I always thought the homes I built were going to be my legacy to the world—they would be here in a hundred years, sheltering families and marking the passing seasons. Well, it doesn't matter anymore, because seven years ago today, at 2:26 in the morning, I realized that you were my real legacy to the world, Angie. You're so special, and I'm exceptionally proud of you. You'll make your mark on this planet, kiddo. I know it. People will be standing in line to thank me for having you.

Happy birthday, Angela. I love you.

Dad

Chapter One

Lenore Pettit slid out of the driver's seat of her car and stood on the crushed stones forming the small parking area behind Paul McDaniels's home. "Stupid, irresponsible jerk!" she muttered as she slammed the vehicle's door with far more force than necessary.

Slinging her portable computer case strap over her shoulder, Lenore stomped around to the front of the house. "How could he?" she asked the arborvitae shading the side of the house. "How *could* he?" she repeated as she pulled open the second of two front doors—the one that led into the part of the house Paul McDaniels had set aside for the business offices of the construction firm he owned and operated out of his home.

Lenore greeted the only other person there. "Hi. It's the stinking end of the month again and I'm here to do the stinking books."

Barb Klucinszki set the telephone she'd been using back in its cradle. She arched one perfectly plucked eyebrow at Lenore and drawled, "Well, aren't you just a ray of sunshine this beautiful spring morning? If you'll step back outside for just a moment, I'll get out my sunglasses so I'm not blinded by all the light and good cheer you brought in with you."

Lenore set her laptop computer onto a vacant desk and unzipped its carrying case. "Oh, shut up."

Barb gave up any pretense of work. The phone was ringing, but she let the answering machine pick up the call. Sitting back in her chair, Barb eyed Lenore carefully. "Good thing we're such good friends," she commented. "Otherwise, I might take offense at the hostile tone in your voice this morning. I thought I was doing you a favor getting you this job. The books weren't *that* bad to get into order last month, were they?"

Lenore sat behind the desk she'd commandeered and put her hands up in surrender. "Okay, okay, I'm way out of line. I know. And no, things were only mildly screwed up here last month. It's not that."

"Then what?" Barb prodded.

"It's just that he's such a complete and total fool. I'm telling you, Barb, there are times when I'm amazed he remembers how to breathe, let alone handle walking and chewing gum at the same time."

Barb leaned forward. "Ooh, we're going to do some serious male bashing. I love it." She straightened her posture. "I'm good at this. Just give me a hint. Who're we going after? Paul?"

Lenore had her laptop plugged in and booted up. Her keystroking stopped, though, with Barb's guess. "Paul?" she questioned. "Paul who?"

Barb rolled her eyes and, when the phone rang, let the answering machine kick in for this next call, as well. "Paul McDaniels," she explained patiently. "The man in whose office you are currently taking up space. What did he do to you? Did he majorly screw up big time? Are we about to be in hot water with the IRS or something?"

Lenore gave her friend a disgusted look. "You have an overactive imagination," she informed her. "And I met Mr. McDaniels the day I interviewed for the job three months ago. Other than that, he hasn't spoken two words to me. He's almost always out on a site someplace when I'm here." And that was the truth. The few times Paul McDaniels had been in the office while Lenore was there, he'd been intent on finding paperwork he needed and had barely acknowledged Lenore's presence. Not that it bothered her to be ignored by such a prime specimen of the opposite sex. Not at all. Hadn't she sworn off men for life after her divorce had finally gone through? It was just that Paul was so large, he was hard to miss when he was taking up any of the precious space that was at such a premium in the tiny office. That was all. Actually, Lenore would have noticed *any* large object in the cramped space. A big rock, for example. Which brought to mind her ex-husband's head and the reason for her bad temper this morning.

"All right, so it's not Paul. Then who?"

As though it were a crystal ball, Lenore gazed thoughtfully into her blank computer screen. "You know, I'm woman enough to admit I made a mistake marrying Richard. I was young, he was a big, macho football player, a real BMOC."

"Sorry," Barb interrupted. "A what?"

"You know, a Big Man on Campus. I couldn't believe an upperclassman—a hotshot football player at that—was paying attention to me. How was I to know the female juniors and seniors already had him figured out as the A-number-one manipulator he is?"

"You couldn't have," Barb soothed. She'd left her desk and was over in a corner of the room plugging in the coffeemaker. Obviously she figured it was going to be a long morning.

"He needed someone to admire his biceps and take care of all the details of running his life for him. I was dumb enough to do it for five years, I admit it," Lenore confessed.

Barb measured out the coffee and ran water into the coffeemaker's reservoir. "As you said, a mistake."

"A big one."

"Well, these things happen. You just have to pick up the pieces and go on."

"I keep trying, darn it. But Richard just won't let me get on with my life." The frustration was back in her voice, but there was little she could do about it. She considered herself fortunate she had enough control left at that point to refrain from flinging herself on the floor and pitching a good old-fashioned hissy fit.

Barb delivered a cup of coffee to her, then prudently went back behind her desk with her own.

Lenore sourly acknowledged to herself that Barb had given herself both distance and something to duck behind should Lenore start throwing things around the room. Well, who knew? She just might need both before the morning was over.

"So, what's he done now?" Barb asked once she was safe.

"It's Timmy," Lenore confessed, cautiously sipping the hot coffee.

"What about him?"

Lenore slammed her fist down on the desk as she thought about it again. Her drink jumped in its mug and she realized a good scalding was a real possibility if she didn't regain her composure. "Oh, sometimes I wish he'd just drop right off the face of the earth."

Barb blinked at that. "You wish your darling little boy would disappear? Boy, things must really be bad. What happened?"

"Not him," Lenore corrected grouchily. "I'm back on his father, Richard. Although I have to tell you, I get extremely depressed every time I think about Timmy growing up and becoming—one of those."

"You mean a man?"

Lenore nodded. "Exactly."

"Hmm."

Lenore typed in a few figures, but her fingers stalled almost immediately. "You know how Timmy is dinosaur crazy?"

"What little boy isn't?" Barb asked with a shrug.

Lenore nodded in agreement. It was one of life's universals. All little boys went nuts over dinosaurs. Someday, scientists would discover a dinosaur gene on the Y chromosome, Lenore was sure. "The third grade did a dinosaur unit a few months ago."

"I bet Timmy loved that," Barb said.

"Yes, he did," Lenore agreed. "But the teacher made the mistake of telling them about this place out in Utah somewhere. Dinosaur National Monument."

"Never heard of it," Barb confessed.

"Me, neither." The phone rang. "You really ought to answer that, you know," she told Barb when her friend made no move to pick up the receiver. "Paul's going to get complaints, and you'll be in hot water."

"Paul would be lost without me," Barb informed her as she finished off her drink. "He needs me too badly to fire me."

"Oh, great. Another dependent male."

"I didn't mean it that way, but never mind. It's more important for you to get whatever's bugging you off your mind. There's steam coming out of your ears, and I think your brain is about to blow. Now what about this place in Utah?"

"Well, this is hard to believe, but a few million years back, the Rocky Mountains were flat as a pancake— plains. And the whole area was lousy with dinosaurs."

"No kidding."

"I kid you not. Evidently, a lot of the little beggars died alongside this prehistoric, long-gone river and got washed downstream only to get snagged by a sandbar where the river took a turn. Timmy's teacher told him the ones that got covered over quickly enough with mud and stuff became fossilized. Then the Rocky Mountains pushed themselves up right through that exact area and the upheaval exposed the entire mess. Timmy tells me that one whole wall of the visitor center of this park is actually the side of a mountain with all kinds of prehistoric bones sticking out in the open and paleontologists working on them right there in front of you."

"Cool."

"Timmy is dying to go there."

"Naturally."

"His father promised to take him as soon as school lets out for the summer."

"Timmy will love that."

"Yeah, well, the twit called me to renege, right as I was leaving this morning. As usual when he's promised to do something, life's circumstances have conspired to make it impossible for him to follow through on his promise. This time I believe his company just got a major order for some specialized machines for a factory in Hong Kong. In order to make the deadline, nobody's being allowed any time off for the next three and a half months."

"Oh, wow. Tough. Right when school starts back up."

Lenore nodded and tapped her finger thoughtfully on the desk top. "It's almost like he paid somebody off, you know? It all just falls into place for him a little too neatly." Lenore shrugged. "But the kicker is, he refuses to tell Timmy himself, so guess who gets to break the news to that poor child who's been looking forward to this for so long?"

"Men," Barb humphed sympathetically.

"What am I going to do?" Lenore wailed as she pushed her laptop out of the way and buried her head in her hands. "For weeks, Timmy hasn't talked about anything else but this trip."

"Well, now, let's think about this logically," Barb said. "You were probably hoping for Timmy to have some quality time with his dad. But realistically, spending all that time with Richard is going to show Timmy even sooner than normal what a jerk his father is."

"True," Lenore admitted. "Very true."

"As satisfying as that would be, it wouldn't be very kind. The obvious solution is for you to take him yourself. There's no real reason why you can't, is there?''

Lenore froze. "Excuse me?"

"You heard me. You take him."

"Listen here, Barbara Louise. Timmy's also got his heart set on the camping part of this trip. *Camping,* do you understand? I do not sleep out in the open. I have always believed that God invented houses and indoor plumbing for a reason.''

"Oh, come on. We're only talking about a couple of weeks here. You can handle that.''

Lenore vehemently denied any such possibility. "No way! There are bears just running around loose out there.'' She nodded her head as she agreed with herself. "Yes, bears. And, and—other wild things. The day they screen in one of the national forests, my friend, is the day I'll consider sleeping out in the open.''

"Oh, come on. Millions of people go camping every year. Probably no more than a mere handful, if that, get attacked by bears. You just have to remember to keep the food out of the tent, I think. Especially at night.''

Rising from her seat, Lenore began to pace and gesture in an agitated fashion. "There has to be some other solution to this. I'm telling you, camping is one of those manly things where a bunch of macho lunkheads think they have to meet nature on its own turf and prove they can still triumph over the elements. Believe me when I tell you that I know where my strengths lie and communing with Mother Nature is not high on the list. Why, I've yet to toast a marshmallow that didn't end up catching fire and turning black, for crying out loud. Forget it.''

Somewhere in the back of the house, a door slammed shut. Lenore looked to Barb. "Who—"

"Jiggers," Barb interrupted. "It's the cops." She pulled a sheaf of papers in front of her and gestured to the desk where Lenore had set up shop. "Sit down and look busy. It's got to be Paul."

And speaking of things ursine, no more than two minutes later, a great bear of a man entered the room. Paul McDaniels was built on a scale that would put Lenore's college-football-playing former husband in the shade in the unlikely event the two found themselves side by side. And Lenore hated whatever self-destructive, perverse part of her nature it was that was responsible for sending her heartbeat into double time and giving her pulse fits right then.

You must be a very shallow person, she lectured herself, *to be so easily suckered once again by nothing more than a guy's looks.*

To be fair to herself and her racing pulse, Paul had those looks in spades. In fact, she wondered if his parents had somehow known the stature he would reach. Perhaps he'd been named after the legendary Paul Bunyan? His legs were like trunks and they ate up the distance from the door into the center of the office space with two large steps. Worn, snug jeans handled the movement with no problem, Lenore thought as she admired their fit across buns tight enough to die for.

It was May and already warm. Paul had teamed a plain white T-shirt with the faded workman's jeans. Biceps rivaling Arnold Schwarzenegger's were blatantly displayed below the short sleeves. A wild red beard covered the lower half of his face, and somehow Lenore just knew it was not a cover-up for a weak chin. Far more likely, it was camouflage to at least cut back on the number of women that must drop at his feet when he walked into a room. Even now, with the beard, that chiseled nose, those blue, blue eyes—oh God, oh God, she had to get a grip.

Quiet, refined, classical-music-loving Lenore Pettit was being turned on by the quintessential macho male. The carpenter's belt with the hammer and other tools of his trade riding low on his hips was killing her. It was then Lenore knew she had a serious genetic flaw for, with all the experience she'd had with this over-size breed of man, she still couldn't catch her breath at the sight of him.

Fortunately for her—she guessed—Paul never seemed to notice her. It was hard to describe, but he would nod, recognize that there was a spare body in the room, but then he would sort of look right through her. Today was no exception.

"Ladies," he said, initiating the ritual.

"Paul," they returned.

But instead of his efficiently taking care of whatever business had brought him in from his current work site and leaving, the ritual deviated.

"I'm in serious trouble this morning," he announced. "I'm in desperate need of help."

While it was true Lenore had only recently added McDaniels Construction to the round of small businesses she helped with their books each month, surely she would have caught an error large enough to bring the IRS down on Paul's head. And, unless she'd been given the wrong figures, she didn't think it could be bankruptcy. But why else would he come to his book-keepers with whatever this major problem was?

Lenore exchanged wide-eyed glances with Barb. Both of them turned to Paul.

Cautiously, and with one hand casually covering the blinking message light on the answering machine, Barb inquired, "Um, what sort of problem is it, Paul?"

"I need a muumuu by nine o'clock tomorrow morning. That only gives me this afternoon to find one. Does either one of you have any ideas where I can get ahold of one?"

"You need a muumuu?" Lenore repeated carefully. Somehow she had trouble picturing him in one. "*You* need a muumuu?"

Those intense blue eyes seized her like a bird of prey with a mouse in sight.

Lenore was immediately sorry she'd opened her mouth.

"Not me personally, no. Angela needs it. You know where I can get one?"

Angela. He had a girlfriend. How nice. No, that was *not* depression she was feeling. "Well, Indiana is a little far removed from the Pacific. But I think I saw a Hawaiian shop in downtown Chicago last time I was there, although I've never seen anything around here in South Bend. Have you, Barb?"

"No. Not that I recall."

"Well, I can't get to Chicago in time to get to this place."

"It's okay," Lenore assured him. "I don't remember exactly where it is anyway."

"Terrific," the big man grunted and ran his fingers through his hair.

"Uh, Paul?" Barb cleared her throat. "Why does Angie need a muumuu? This is May. Halloween's in October."

He stopped in his tracks and glared. "I know that. I just found out this morning that the first grade has been studying Hawaii. They're celebrating the end of the unit with a pretend luau tomorrow, and they're all supposed to come in Hawaiian dress."

Paul's books were never going to get done at this rate, Lenore thought as she lost her place once more. Well, at least he wasn't about to be hauled in front of the IRS. He should be grateful for that much, at least. She, of course, was *not* grateful to discover that Angie must be his daughter rather than his girlfriend. She'd gotten the impression from Barb that Paul wasn't married, but if he had a daughter, the child had a mother. Let *her* take care of Angie's costume.

Lenore had never seen any sign of a woman's touch around the place. God knew the room she currently sat in could use a bit of wallpaper or a touch of color *somewhere* in the place.

Paul and his wife must be divorced, she decided. Maybe Angie's mother had moved out of state; maybe that was why Paul had such a desperate look about him. Well, none of it made any difference to her. When it came to men, Lenore was suspicious, not sympathetic. "Are you sure you didn't know about this until this morning? I doubt any school would expect parents to come up with a muumuu in a single day."

Paul glared at her once again.

Lenore shivered and shrank back in her chair, sorry she'd asked.

"I have no idea how long the note has been aging in the bottom of Angie's backpack. I only know it was presented to me just this morning. I have to come up with a dozen coconut cupcakes and a muumuu by nine tomorrow morning. Now can either one of you help me or not?"

This was a truly agitated man, Lenore decided. His hair was always on the wild side, but now it was starting to stick up in spikes, he'd run his hand through it so often in the past five minutes.

Determinedly, she clamped her lips shut. This was not her problem. Let the macho man whip up a muumuu for his daughter. She'd been taken advantage of often enough in her short marriage, she was absolutely not going to get involved—not ever again. In fact, Lenore had every intention of training herself to like wimpy, introverted types. The kind that had plastic pocket protectors in their shirt pockets. If it wasn't a contradiction in terms, a male with small-muscle coordination who could handle a needle and sew his own buttons back on. That would—

"Lenore knows how to sew."

What? Lenore gazed aghast at her—from this point on—former friend.

Imperturbably, Barb ignored her. "Honestly, she sews all kinds of things. You should just see the Halloween costumes her son turns up in year after year. Why, I bet it wouldn't take Lenore more than a couple of hours to come up with a muumuu, especially one that little."

Lenore was going to kill Barb. She really was. Just as soon as she could think of some rotten enough method to do the trick. Lenore wouldn't want it to be anything too quick or painless.

"Oh, I really don't think I have the time—"

But Paul was already whipping out his wallet from his back pocket. "How much do you think you'll need? I'll pay anything."

It was imperative to show no sign of weakness. She'd learned that lesson relatively late in life, but she had learned it. "I'm sorry, Paul, but I already have plans for this evening." See how easy it could be, she congratulated herself. Her response had been succinct, to the point and deliberately vague. Paul could have no comeback. And best of all, it wasn't even a lie. She had told Timmy—

"Oh, come on, Lenore. Timmy will understand if you explain this is sort of an emergency. He doesn't even need the baseball mitt until this weekend anyway."

That had come out of Barb's mouth! Lenore's head swung in amazement to stare at her friend. Why was Barb doing everything in her power to push Lenore into this? Obviously she had some kind of hidden agenda. Possibly she was suicidal and bent on pushing Lenore into taking care of the deed for her? That way, her insurance would still pay off. Lenore certainly could see her way to fulfilling her friend's subconscious death wish, if that was the case.

She spoke firmly, knowing it would be all the defense she had for her now-exposed flimsy excuse. "I think Timmy has had to deal with enough broken promises in his eight short years, don't you?"

Barb shrugged. "Sure, but this is different. Timmy would understand a valid reason for switching nights. That's different from Richard just backing out on the dates he makes with Tim for no good reason." Ingeniously, Barb added, "And you could take him with you. I'm sure that if Paul were to offer to throw in, say, a trip through the Golden Arches for some take-out on his way to your place tonight, it might go a long way to assuage any feelings of neglect Timmy might feel.''

''Barb...''

Paul slowly stuffed his wallet back into his back pocket. ''You're divorced? A single parent? I didn't know.''

How could he know? The miserable excuse of a hunk of a man before her had never—not once in the three months she'd been working there—noticed her. Now that he knew she could sew, suddenly he was Mr. Attentive. Life really stunk.

Paul continued, ''I guess you've already got your hands full. Look, just forget it, okay? I'll think of something.'' Paul paced for a minute, head bowed. ''All right, how about this? One of those brown pa-per grocery bags with the bottom cut out and the sides all shredded with scissors. That would look like a grass skirt if I wrap it around her middle and tape it some-how, wouldn't it?'' He snapped his fingers. ''I know, a pillowcase. They make them with flowers on them, don't they? She's determined to have flowers for some reason. Cut a hole for the head, two more for the arms. I did a pretty good ghost like that a couple of Halloweens ago.''

''Lenore, please—I saw that ghost costume,'' Barb pleaded.

Oh, this was too pathetic for words. And he prob-ably knew he was playing on her sympathies. Oh heck, it was working. Lenore slapped the desk top with both hands and jumped out of her chair as she capitulated. ''Okay, okay! I'll do it.''

"No, it's—"

"Wait till you meet Angie. She's so cute. You should have had a daughter. They're so much more fun than boys to sew for...."

This was ridiculous. Any daughter of that mountain over there would not be cute. Paul made a great-looking guy, fabulous to really be objective about it, but she had trouble envisioning him in a dress. The idea of some poor little—make that large—seven-year-old trying to be feminine while learning to cope with a body the size of Paul's was what had really captured her sympathy. "I said I'd do it!"

"What's wrong with the pillowcase idea? That was a great ghost."

There was no doubt in Lenore's mind that it was poor form to yell like a banshee in one's place of employment, especially when the screaming was directed at one's employer, but, hey, after twenty-seven years of always being the good, polite little girl, it felt great. "Quiet! Do you hear me? I want absolute quiet in this room."

Paul McDaniels was not used to being spoken to in that fashion. It showed in the expression on his face. "I was only trying—" he started.

"Not another word." Lenore walked around her desk and approached Paul. She poked him right in the chest. It was like granite. "I have work to do here," she informed the rock. "Books to catch up on, payroll to get out. I want you out of here so I can concentrate. Go build something."

"But Angie—"

"Will be in a pillowcase if I don't get this done by five o'clock. By the way, be back here by then. You'll be paying me ten dollars an hour for my time this eve-

ning. I'm sure you won't want to waste any of it."
That'll make him stop and take notice, she thought in
satisfaction.

"Ten dollars an hour? For a little bit of sewing?"

"You want to do it?"

"I'll be here."

Chapter Two

How had he not noticed the little spitfire working in his office? Paul pondered the question as he helped the delivery-truck driver unload drywall at the site he was trying to ready for the Panorama of Homes, which opened in two weeks. If he and everybody else he employed worked their butts off between now and then, he just might make it. He hefted another sheet.

"Frank, grab those drywall nails and bring them down to Todd. You two got the studs up in the basement this morning, right? I want the drywall up and the first coat of mud started by late this afternoon."

"We ran short on tenpenny nails. Had to make a hardware run, but no sweat, Todd's down there finishing up now."

Paul grunted his acknowledgment while he heaved the heavy drywall the rest of the way off the truck. He'd known Barb had hired someone to come in a few days a month to help her out. Hell, he'd even talked to the woman—what was her name? Lenore, yeah, Lenore—briefly himself before giving her the okay. Lenore.

Pretty name.

Pretty woman.

Which brought him back to the first point. What was the matter with him that he was just noticing her now? After he'd married Amanda, he'd still *noticed* other women. It had stopped right there, of course. Admittedly he'd been through a lot since Amanda's death and those good times had ended, but, hell's bells, he was only thirty-two years old. How could his libido be dead already? And if it had withered away without his realizing, it seemed grossly unfair. What was he supposed to do with the rest of his life—join a monastery? He didn't know too many monks with kids. Damn, it wasn't dead. It couldn't be dead. It had just been sick for a while, that was it.

He stacked his load against the open studwork of the newly framed-out garage wall. They'd have to get the drywall up and taped in here, as well, he thought as he went back for two more sheets.

He stretched his arms up behind his back in an effort to work the kinks out of his muscles and breathed deeply. Damn, was there anything better than the smell of fresh sawdust in the air?

Unless it was the erotic scent of a woman's natural perfume. Oh, yes, at one time he'd been quite a connoisseur of the opposite sex. But he'd fallen hard for Amanda and never felt the need to roam after that. God, he'd loved that woman.

"Almost done," the driver called to Paul as he reached the truck.

"Can't wait to take off, huh? I'm crushed."

"Hey, I got a load of two-by-fours to get out by two o'clock this afternoon."

"No rest for the wicked, I guess."

The older man chortled. "You got that right, and I was bad in my prime. Real bad. Man, those were the days. The ladies used to love me, and I loved them in return. Now I just wish I had a penny for every piece of lumber I've lugged on or off this thing."

Paul had heard it before. He filled in the blank. "You'd be a wealthy man, right?"

"Yes, sir. Yes, sir." The man straightened up after shoving the last fifty-pound bucket of taping compound into the garage area. "Well, that about does it. Be seeing you."

Paul touched his forehead with two fingers in a brief salute. "Yeah." Squinting in the sunlight, he watched the other man climb into the truck cab and take off down the road. Dust laid down by the many construction vehicles moving through the new subdivision swirled up behind the truck. Paul loved it. He loved everything to do with making a barren tract of land habitable, bringing it to life. Why, in a few weeks when the Panorama opened, all the houses on both sides of this street would be finished, ready for families to move right in and create an instant neighborhood.

Paul wondered who would buy the house he was currently building. There'd been a young engaged couple through last week, but he'd heard they'd bought one across the street and down a few—and that house was now the only one on the block sporting a sold sign.

Yes, his business was fascinating. Paul wouldn't change it for anything in the world. He loved his work.

He loved life, or at least he always had.

It worried him that Lenore had been right there under his nose for—how long? He scratched the cheek under his beard as he thought. Had to be at least a couple of months. Maybe more. He didn't even know! What did that say about his mental state of well-being?

Yes, he'd been devastated when Amanda had died four years ago, but Amanda wouldn't have wanted him to mourn too long. She'd have wanted him to pick up the pieces and get on with life. Everyone at the funeral had said so. Of course, Amanda had been an extremely caring, giving kind of person. Had the shoe been on the other foot, Paul doubted he would have been nearly so generous with any good wishes for a spouse's speedy recovery from grief and a quick as well as happy new life with someone else. He wanted to be mourned when he went. For a good long time. Would twenty or thirty years in black be asking too much for a man such as himself tragically cut down in the prime of his life? He thought not.

But as much as he'd loved and still missed Amanda, his grief had moved with time to the back burners of his mind. Now he was just plain lonely. And he was still worried over what appeared to be a four-year-long blank-out.

Yes, his business had kept him busy.

Yes, he'd had to concentrate on being both mother and father to Angie—and believe you him, picking out little-girl dresses was not his forte.

As far as Paul was concerned, those were not credible excuses. Paul shrugged. Well, too late to worry now. He hadn't even realized anything was amiss until signs of his recovery had hit him over the head in the form of one recalcitrant but shapely bookkeeper.

He'd noticed her. He'd check her out in more detail tonight. The monastery would have to make do without him.

Paul entered the house through the garage and proceeded down the basement stairs. Time to instill a little fear into these guys if this place was going to be finished in time.

Paul worked like a madman for the rest of the day. Not wanting to stop for lunch, he'd bled all over a new wall when he'd sliced his finger open trying to juggle eating a sandwich with cutting drywall. The drywall knife had won. But he packed it in at four-thirty. He picked Angie up from the after-school day care provided by the school, and by two minutes after five, his truck was rolling to a stop in the parking area next to his house.

Lenore was already waiting and glancing impatiently at her wristwatch.

"She better not start harping about two lousy minutes," Paul muttered. "Not with what I've been through today."

"What have you been through, Daddy?" Angie asked as she peered bright-eyed through the windshield at Lenore.

"You don't want to know."

"Is that the lady who's gonna make my muu-muu?"

"I hope so."

"She looks nice."

Lenore looked a lot of things, Paul decided as he studied her critically. Sexy as hell, for one, what with the way the spring breeze was blowing wisps of hair around her face and molding her blouse to what appeared from here to be a pair of mighty fine breasts.

"Nice" remained to be seen. The way he'd been feeling all afternoon, it would suit his purposes just fine
if she didn't turn out to be *too* nice.

This couldn't be Paul's daughter, Lenore thought in
amazement as a pigtailed sprite jumped down from the
cab of Paul's pickup. Paul was so darn masculine,
she'd admittedly had trouble imagining a feminized
version of him. But regardless of how nebulous her
vision had been, one thing she'd been sure of—that
particular genetic code trying for ladylike—well, it was
a recipe for disaster, that's what it was.

Half the reason Lenore had allowed herself to be
coerced into doing this was because she felt sorry for
any little girl of his. The poor thing would no doubt be
heads taller than anyone else her age. Lenore pictured
Paul's progeny as gawky, gangly and awkward—the
overly large, pitiable stepsister trying to squeeze her
size-ten foot into Cinderella's delicate, petite glass
slipper.

This kid was downright diminutive—a cute little
button of a child with her father's bright blue eyes and
freckles splattered all across the bridge of her nose.
And she obviously liked being out-of-doors. School
was still in session, but Paul's daughter's cheeks were
pinkened from the sun and already slightly peeling.
She would have to speak to Paul about sunscreen, but
at least a daughter with a love of the outdoors fitted
her image of the man.

Lenore had imagined Paul's child with wild red hair
that made her cry when a brush got dragged through
it. She'd be in despair over her inability to tame it
when she hit junior high.

This diminutive elf had straight, shiny hair such a
dark shade of brown it verged on black. Pulled back

on either side from an almost but not quite straight
center part, her hair was neatly caught up in two long
pigtails that hung silkily over her ears.

She wore jeans and a pink oxford-cloth shirt, but
the shirt was neatly tucked in, and on her feet she had
miniversions of Paul's construction boots. Lenore
couldn't even really criticize those. Hey, grunge was in.

In a word, the child was adorable. "You're Angela?" Lenore asked, half-expecting her to deny it.

"I'm Angie," she responded, grinning and pointing to her chest.

Paul's wife had obviously had *very* strong genes.
They'd have had to have been, to wrestle all of Paul's
heavily masculine ones into submission and produce
this—angel.

"And I know who you are, too," Angie exclaimed
proudly.

"Yeah? Who?"

"You're the nice lady who's gonna make me a
muumuu for the party tomorrow."

Paul came up beside his daughter and laid a hand on
her shoulder. "Muumuus take time, angelface, and we
haven't got much of it, so we better get going. We
don't want Mrs. Pettit to be up all night." Paul suspected it wouldn't be at all wise to put Lenore's
"niceness" to the test. Although, for ten bucks an
hour, she ought to at least keep a civil tongue in her
head. Somehow, though, he was not the least bit con-
fident she would see things that way.

It wasn't until Lenore picked up the strap of her
computer case and swung it over her shoulder that
Paul realized he should have carried it for her.

Again he cursed the past four years. His manners
were rusty. Men on a construction site didn't expect

you to hold the door for them or say please and thank-you when you yelled for someone to toss you a hammer.

"I need to swing by my house," Lenore said as she walked briskly to her own car.

She didn't seem upset by his lack of courtliness. Had it been so long since anyone had seen to her needs?

"Timmy stays with a neighbor after school when I'm working away from home, and they'll be expecting me."

The fine points of being around a woman were slowly coming back to him. He should shower. He could be quick about it. "How about if we meet over on Grape Road in thirty minutes? Burgers and fries on me. Angie and I need to clean up a bit, and I haven't got enough seat belts for everyone anyway. It would be best to take two cars."

That interested her. "You make Angie buckle up?"

He turned back from hustling Angie into the house. "Of course she buckles up. Doesn't Timmy?"

So, he was a good, protective father. She didn't like admiring him for it, but she did. "Timmy knows the car doesn't move until his belt is fastened."

"That's what my daddy says, too," Angie piped in. "He says there are a lot of real turkeys out on the roads, and he doesn't want my hard head putting a hole in his good windshield if he has to stop real fast."

Lenore had to grin at that. "That would be bad, all right."

"Yeah," Angie agreed. "He says my freckles would probably get knocked loose, too, and we'd have a heck of a time finding and picking them all up again, I've got so many."

Lenore made a production of inspecting Angie's face. "Daddy's got a point." And just look at Daddy turning red. Her heart softened a bit toward the big, gruff man. Even though he had waited until the last minute to do anything about Angie's muumuu—like you could just waltz into any store in South Bend, Indiana, and pick one up—he was good with his daughter. They obviously spent time teasing and bantering around with each other. He got points for that. Not many, but some.

Ah, well, best to get on with it. "I'll see you there in about half an hour," she said as she unlocked her car door and slid into the driver's seat. Keeping an eye on Angie's whereabouts, she carefully backed up and drove off.

Any way you slice this, she thought as she headed back to her own neighborhood, Timmy was not going to be a happy camper tonight. Not only did the baseball-mitt shopping expedition have to be put off— at least that was only a delay—but canceling the camping trip was going to kill him. God, she hated all men. Paul lost points in her book this afternoon just for being male. So what if he made his daughter buckle up? Big deal. He was supposed to.

But back to Timmy. She might as well tell him now and hope the treat of a fast-food dinner would get him through the roughest part of the initial disappointment. Her sigh was loud in the insulated quiet of the car. This was going to be bad.

And it was.

Timmy tried hard to be brave; she could see the struggle play out across his expressive little face. In fact, his lower lip was still trembling now and again as she pulled underneath the golden arches.

Paul and Angie met them at the entrance.

"Right on time, I see," Paul said as he guided them through the glass doors.

"Of course," Lenore retorted without any real heat. She was too busy watching Timmy's countenance darken further. Having to spend his evening with a yucky girl was, no doubt, the final blow.

Paul seated them all, then went to pick up their order. When he came back to the table, he handed Lenore and Angie their food first, then set out his and Timmy's. "I want to thank you," he told the boy gravely as he handed him a carton of milk, "for delaying picking out your mitt for Angie and me. I was really in a bind, but your mother didn't want to disappoint you. I had to do some serious arm twisting to get her to agree to help me out tonight, but I do feel bad and I'd like to make things up to you."

Lenore was surprised by Paul's apology. In her experience, most men were dense enough that, even had they been told point-blank, they would still not have believed that other people might have their own priorities and needs. Or if, by some remote chance, such an oddball thing should occur, the male mind innately knew that the other person's needs couldn't possibly be as important as his own and was therefore easily relegated to a lesser priority. While Paul had made sure Angie's muumuu came first, at least he was aware of what he'd done. His apology was—interesting.

"It's okay," Timmy muttered as he struggled with his milk carton. His scowling countenance belied his words.

Angie gave her dad her milk. Evidently it was a familiar ritual, for without any words being exchanged,

Paul tugged the top of her container into the spout position and handed it back. In an offhand, natural manner Lenore realized was designed to ensure Timmy knew it was all right to be helped, Paul reached for the boy's carton and fixed it, as well. "It is a big deal and you've been a good sport."

So Paul was a liar, as well.

"Now I don't know your mom real well—yet ..."

Lenore straightened up in her seat. Was that a threat?

"And while it's obvious she's a real smart lady..." he continued.

It was?

"I get the feeling she's more comfortable with other things, uh, more creative-type things than baseball. I heard she's made you some pretty fancy Halloween outfits, for example."

Timmy agreed with that assessment. "Yeah, last year she made me this really cool Power Ranger outfit. It was the best ever." He shook his head mournfully. "But my dad and I learned a long time ago never to go into a fabric store with her. We're going to be stuck in there *all night*. Wait and see. If we go there first, I'll never get my mitt. It takes her forever to make up her mind. She says it's because there're too many choices." Timmy slumped in his seat. "Why do we hafta go with them? Couldn't they go by themselves while we go look at gloves or something?"

Paul shook his head. "Sorry, champ. But a man's gotta do what a man's gotta do. Since Angie's my daughter and my responsibility, I've got to go along for the ride here and help your mother out. But like I said, I'll make it up to you."

Not wanting Paul to misunderstand, Timmy assured him, "I mean, I like my mom and everything, but you're right. She doesn't understand about baseball and how important it is to have the right mitt."

"I understand completely. My own mother used to pick out mitts by price tag, if you can believe that. She always said you shouldn't buy the bottom of the line 'cause it's probably junk. And there was no need to buy the top of the line because you were just paying extra for the name brand or some guy's signature who'd already made a million batting a little ball around with a stick. She'd be darned if he'd get started on his second million by taking advantage of her. No, in my sainted mother's opinion, you went for whichever middle-of-the-road glove was on sale." Paul shook his head in disbelief.

So did Lenore. Wasn't that how it was done? And she was feeling, um, left out, she guessed.

Left out? How ridiculous. "That's how you get the most for your money, isn't it?" she asked, determined to be a part of the conversation. What was wrong with her? Who wanted to be part of a conversation about baseball gloves?

She did. Why? Because Paul was involved in discussing them. How sad.

Paul looked at her askance. "Lenore, there's a lot more to be considered here than just price. For example, you've got to check how deep the pocket is and whether the back strap is padded or not. I still remember the year I actually had to use a *vinyl* glove because it was ten dollars cheaper than real leather."

"No." Timmy breathed the word in horror.

"What's wrong with that?" Lenore asked.

Paul merely rolled his eyes. "Everything," he said. "I was totally mortified in front of all the guys, for one thing. But here's what I was thinking. I played an awful lot of ball growing up, and I know a thing or two about picking out a good mitt. I wonder if you'd let me come along on Saturday morning when you go shopping? Been a long time since I punched a good piece of leather."

This was fascinating, Lenore thought as she rested her chin on her hand. One of those guy things you heard so much about. There was Paul, sitting in his seat across from her, letting his fries get cold while he punched his right fist into his open left hand just the way Timmy did when he tried on a baseball glove. Timmy said doing that was like pretending the ball was smacking into the glove and it gave him a feel for the mitt. What a lot of mystical male—hooey. But there was her son, eating it right up. She supposed she ought to be grateful. The child whose life might as well have been over no more than an hour ago appeared to be experiencing a miraculous recovery. "Since my opinion is obviously going to be considered extraneous anyway, why don't you two go without me? Angie and I can look at fabric by ourselves."

"Yeah, great, that would really be wicked, right, Paul?"

Lenore had not gone into parenting totally naive. She'd known there would be times when the best interests of her child would directly conflict with her own best interests. She just hadn't realized how frequently these situations would pop up. Take her current situation.

Please.

She and Timmy were becoming more and more embroiled with Paul and his daughter with every second that ticked by. She did not want to spend any more time with this man than was absolutely necessary. He was an impediment to her peace of mind. Maybe if she sent them off to get a mitt, she could use the time in the fabric store to whip herself back into shape. There was little doubt in her mind that without her guidance, Timmy would come home with a solid gold mitt, but to regain her equilibrium, it would be worth the extra expense.

"Nope," Paul said, much to Lenore's surprise. "A man doesn't shirk his responsibilities."

He didn't?

"I'm not sticking you with the work while I go off and have fun. First we take care of the muumuu, then the mitt. Right, Tim?"

"Uh..."

"Paul, this really isn't necessary."

But Paul wouldn't hear any more about it. "Nope, what's right is right. I just kind of got distracted there for a minute. Baseball does that to me. That major league strike a couple of years ago about killed me. I have to admit it."

His daughter rolled her eyes. "My dad's really bad about baseball, Mrs. Pettit. He doesn't even care what teams are playing, he'll watch it anyways. And he yells at the TV like the playermen can hear him. I keep telling him they can't really, but..." Angie shrugged meaningfully.

Lenore patted her hand. "I understand, dear." But she didn't. What woman truly understood men and their sports? Armies of doctoral candidates could write theses on the topic and hardly make a dent, she was sure. "You and I will make it our job to keep them on task tonight, all right?"

Angie happily slipped her hand into Lenore's. "Okay. Can we go now? This is going to be so much fun. I want flowers on my dress. Big white ones. And lots of them."

Angie continued to chatter cheerfully as they made their way across the parking lot that separated the restaurant from a large strip mall that included a fabric store.

Forty-five minutes later, Lenore knew she'd been caught up in a three-ring circus. Both Paul and Timmy were determined to help, but trying to deal with the suggestions coming at her from all sides only made Lenore want to scream for a different kind of help entirely.

"Look, baby doll, how about this one? It's got a ruffle around the bottom," Paul said, pointing to a drawing in the pattern book. "Oh, it's blue. Never mind. You don't like blue."

"Try to remember we're only looking at the style of the dress right now. These are just examples. We can make Angie's dress whatever color we want."

"With big flowers!" the child insisted.

"If they have some fabric like that," Lenore agreed.

Timmy sank lower in the chair next to Lenore. His legs were spread wide and sprawled out in front of him. They were all that kept him from slipping out of the chair entirely. "We're never going to get out of here," he predicted glumly. "Not ever. I showed you about a hunnert pictures of dresses already and you haven't choosed one yet."

"I happen to remember exactly how long it took you to pick out that last baseball mitt, young man, so don't you go giving Angie or me any grief. Look here, Angie. This one's called a stitch-in-time pattern. That means I can make it quickly. You can wear it to school tomorrow with a shirt underneath, and then when it's really hot, you can use it for a sundress. What do you say?''

Angie scrunched up her nose as she studied the picture Lenore showed her. ''We can make it out of flowers, right?''

''Absolutely,'' Lenore agreed. ''And I think if we bought some of those silk flowers over there, we might have time to make you a lei.''

''Okay,'' the child said happily.

Paul jumped up, grateful for something more active to do and, using the number in the book, located the pattern in its drawer.

''All we need now is the fabric,'' Lenore said, pleased with their progress.

Twenty minutes later, Paul paid for their selections. He'd only blanched a little when given the total amount. Sewing was not necessarily cheaper than buying ready-made. You had to wait for the sales, which, of course, working under the gun like this, was not possible. Angie clutched her purchases to her chest the moment the clerk tucked the receipt into the bag and tried to hand it to Paul.

''I'll be in charge of the bag,'' she announced as she pivoted and hurried toward the door. ''Come on, Dad. Mrs. Pettit says we've got a lot to do.''

''I'm right behind you, pumpkin,'' he said, which was a lie as he was still standing at the counter replacing his credit card and sliding his wallet into the back pocket of his jeans.

Lenore looked longingly around as they prepared to leave. "I hate going into fabric stores," she commented.

Paul gave her a quizzical glance. "What's to hate about it?" he asked, escorting her out. "It's not exactly a guy kind of place, but if you're half as creative as Barb says you are, you ought to be in nirvana here."

"My car's over there," Lenore said, pointing it out. "You can just follow me to my house, I guess."

"Come on, Angie," Paul said and struck out across the parking lot. "That's my truck just a few spaces down from you. You didn't answer my question."

Lenore shrugged as they walked. "I never end up even after a trip there."

Paul mulled that over for a bit. He gave up. "Excuse me?"

Lenore gestured with both hands up in front of her. Her right hand went out palm up. "Okay, take tonight. We went in there for a pattern that would do for a muumuu and two yards of fabric. That's all."

Paul nodded. "I'm with you so far. And that's just what we got. A pattern and two yards of fabric. Oh, also some elastic. Was that what you meant?"

"No, no." Lenore reached for the backs of both children's shirts and tugged the youngsters to a halt. "Watch what you're doing, you two. That car's got its back-up lights on. Wait and see if he's paying attention before you walk behind it." She turned back to Paul. "No, while I was there I saw this really cute pattern for a skirt."

He was intrigued in spite of himself. "So why didn't you buy it?"

"I don't need it. So I was brave and left it there."

"Uh-huh." He boosted Angie into the cab of the truck, slammed the door, and turned again to Lenore.

"But sooner or later I'll break down and go back and get it."

He'd seen that one coming. He hadn't been married before for nothing. "Yeah?"

She nodded. "I can only be strong for so long."

"Right."

"And once I cave in and buy the pattern, I'll have to choose some fabric, but there will be more than one piece of material that I'll fall in love with. I'll have to return to the pattern books to find something to make out of the other one. Once I'm back looking through those—"

"I get the idea. You never end up even."

She looked pleased with his quickness. "Yes."

And to think he'd been letting this woman monkey around with his bookkeeping system the past few months. Paul couldn't help but wonder how she went about balancing all those little columns of numbers if they didn't add up quite right. Lord help him.

He tried to be generous. "I suppose it's something like me when I get into a hardware store. Go for a screwdriver, and an hour later, Angie's ripping out her hair she's so bored and I've picked up a basketful of stuff I probably could get along fine without."

"Oh, it's nothing like a hardware store," Lenore assured him. "I have no problem there. Go in for a screwdriver, come out with a screwdriver. I never understood my father's fascination with tools and things. Either you need it or you don't. Now patterns and materials are different. They involve choices and visualizing how different styles and colors will look."

He saw Lenore into her car and shut the door, then waited while she rolled down the window. "Okay, fine. It's nothing like the hardware store. I would like to point out, however, that screwdrivers come in several different styles, lengths and thicknesses." He had her here. "They also have different colored handles. Black, yellow, sometimes even red. I've got to make choices, too." He laughed at her look of disbelief. Amanda had been like that. Totally unable to understand the male fascination for a good home improvement center. "Just do me a favor and don't lose me on the way to your place, okay?" He didn't wait for her response.

Chapter Three

Lenore sighed as she drove down the road, Paul's headlights bobbling in her rearview mirror. Only a man would—or even could—equate a hardware store with a fabric shop. Lenore frowned so severely her eyebrows came close to pinching together over the bridge of her nose. Men had no soul, that was the problem. Although, for a man, Paul certainly had exhibited some very bizarre behavior tonight. She'd offered to let him off the hook and go mitt shopping with Timmy, and instead of jumping at the opportunity, he'd declined, and most emphatically. Now what had that been all about? Most unmacho-like behavior if you asked her.

"What's the matter, Mom?" Timmy searched her face in the dark of the car for the meaning hidden behind the sigh and frown. "You don't have to worry about the mitt, you know. I don't really expect Mr. McDaniels to come with us. The two of us can get it

Saturday morning by ourselves. I know he's your boss
and all, so you couldn't say no, and besides, the hamburger was good. Mr. McDaniels bought large fries,
too, instead of small, so it was worth it."

Oh, damn Richard anyway, Lenore silently raged.
Look how Timmy automatically assumed Paul was
going to back out of the commitment he'd made. "I
don't know him very well, but Mr. McDaniels seems
to be a man of his word," Lenore tried to assure her
son. Paul better be, or she would personally snip everything in his wardrobe and make grass skirts out of
them. He'd be there Saturday morning if Lenore had
to go pull him out of bed and dress him herself.

Hmm, now there was a thought. Did Paul sleep in
the buff? That was a thought definitely worth thinking about.

Disgusted with herself for such prurient thoughts,
Lenore put on her signal light and pulled into her
driveway. Paul's headlights followed right behind.

"I hope you put your cereal bowl in the sink the way
I told you to when we left this morning," she told her
son as they approached the back door, the house key
in her hand.

"Yeah, sure," Timmy said before ducking his head
while he tried to recall for sure. "I think."

Lenore rolled her eyes. Good grief. She was about
to bring that incredible hunk of a man into a dirty
kitchen.

She froze as she realized the direction her thoughts
had taken. See? Was she becoming depraved? Now
was not the time for her body to start making de-
mands of its own. Not with a man like Paul Mc-
Daniels in the immediate vicinity. She just had to keep
telling herself that sexual attraction was the *only* area

of agreement between the sexes. Sure, they wanted each other, but men and women were entirely too incompatible to stay together for very long. Of that small but pertinent fact, Lenore had personal experience.

It was a heck of a situation, Lenore decided as she swung the door open and flicked on the light. She let her gaze dart around the room.

"Guess I remembered, huh, Mom?"

"Good thing," she returned as she took in the empty countertops. Things weren't too bad.

Paul and Angie were hurrying up the sidewalk behind them. There were only a few seconds left for a last minute personal pep talk. Lenore put the time to good advantage. Was she or was she not more than her DNA? Of course she was. She was not a slave to her hormones. And she would prove it tonight. When Paul left later on this evening, she would not give him so much as a passing thought until a month from now when it was time to go back and help Barb again. Lenore scowled. That was if she decided to go back and help Barb, of course. The dirty traitor.

She did not need another man in her life, Lenore reminded herself one last time. She would rise above this, this—mere sexual attraction, and that, dear friend, would be that.

Paul ducked his head at the doorway. Force of habit, she guessed. She thought he would have cleared the opening anyway. Now he was in the kitchen. Her kitchen. Filling it. God, just look how he filled the room with his presence.

Just like Richard, one part of her brain screeched to the other. *Just you keep that in mind. Richard used to fill a room like that.*

Richard hadn't filled a room anything like Paul, the other half of her brain answered right back. In no way, shape or form.

She was in trouble.

The best thing to do, Lenore counseled herself, was to take immediate charge and not let control slip out of her hands for the remainder of the evening. That's all it was, one lousy evening.

"All right, Timmy. You go pick out a movie for Angie to watch while you practice your piano. Your lesson is tomorrow, so make sure you've got that C scale down pat. How about *The Little Mermaid? Aladdin*'s in there someplace, too, but you can't join Angie until you've played for at least twenty minutes, got it?"

Lenore reached for the bag Angie had set on the kitchen counter. The little girl beat her to it. "But I wanna help sew my dress."

Timmy piped up, "And I already practiced this morning."

So much for staying in control.

"Five minutes spent trying to pick out the theme to *Jurassic Park* doesn't count."

"But—"

Lenore raised her hand. "Stop. I haven't got time for an argument tonight. Paul and I have a lot to get done and we need a little cooperation around here." She eyed Paul's daughter. How to get her to hand over the goods she had clutched so tightly to her chest without hurting her feelings? She mulled over her options, angry that it fell to her to do so. Why couldn't men ever take the initiative in situations such as this? Richard had always abdicated his responsibilities by claiming women had a way with children that men did not. This, however, wasn't even her own child. You would think—

"Angie, you have a decision to make here," Paul said, startling Lenore.

He made no attempt to remove the bag from her grasp, Lenore noticed.

"I do?" the child questioned suspiciously.

"Yes," Paul nodded gravely.

From the tone of her voice, it was obvious Angie was searching for the trap. It was just as obvious to Lenore that Paul's reasonable approach had been used before and was familiar to the little girl. It was why Angie was so suspicious right then.

Lenore kept quiet and waited to see how Paul would handle this.

"Because we only have one night to get this done, if you choose to have Lenore..."

It worried her that they were starting to getting on a first-name basis, even in front of the children. It spoke of a familiarity Lenore knew she wasn't ready for.

"...spend her time this evening teaching you how to sew, your muumuu probably won't be finished in time for you to wear it to school tomorrow morning. Lenore, on the other hand, already knows how to sew, and if we stay out of her way and let her get on with it, you'll have a new dress for the luau. Now, how do you want to deal with it?"

Freud couldn't have handled Angie better, Lenore decided in reluctant admiration. All the responsibility had been dumped right back onto Angie, letting Lenore and Paul off the hook. Neither one had to play the big, bad ogre. Amazing.

Clearly, Paul had been to parenting classes or done a lot of reading on the topic. He did not fall into the yelling, screaming, verbally abusive father category Lenore observed so frequently at Timmy's various sport events.

It pleased her. And that made her mad.

Reluctantly, Angie handed over the bag. "Oh, all right, I'll go watch a dumb old movie."

"Fine. And if you decide you want to, I saw a sign at the fabric store for a sewing class for children. We can check into it this weekend."

The child nodded, partially appeased. "Okay."

"All right," Lenore said, restraining herself from giving Paul a high five. That was one battle averted. Maybe they were on a roll. "Listen, pumpkin, your dad and I are going down to the basement to get started. You and Timmy be good, and if you need us, Timmy can show you the way."

Timmy, who had more experience dealing with his mother than Angie, had obviously suspected Paul McDaniels was more of the same. He'd assumed the outcome of the argument would not be in Angie's favor. The opening swell of *The Little Mermaid* was already competing with the plinking of the piano as Lenore led Paul to the basement steps.

"I think your piano needs tuning," Paul commented as they headed down. "A musician friend of mine does it on the side, if you're interested."

"I just had it looked at, thanks."

"You sure the guy knew what he was doing?" Paul asked doubtfully. "I could have Jack double-check. I don't think he'd charge too much if I told him it was for a friend of mine."

She was not his friend. She would never be his friend. It was too dangerous. And that, just like the sun setting into Lake Michigan each night, was a certainty. "It was a woman and she's not the problem. Timmy just started lessons a few weeks ago," Lenore said by way of explanation. "He's not real sure which key is which quite yet. It can get pretty painful around here during practice time. Remind me to have him review his note-reading flash cards when we go back upstairs."

It was fun, Lenore decided twenty minutes later. Having a man under her thumb was definitely a kick. She'd spread out the material on her cutting board, laid out the front and back of the dress, pinned and cut them out while Paul watched. Those in hand, she handed the rest of the pieces to Paul, who eyed her with something akin to panic. It gave Lenore a sense of satisfaction to know she'd put that look there.

"I'm going to start sewing. Your job is to get the rest of this stuff cut out as fast as possible. See how each pattern piece is labeled? When I ask you for the front facing, the bottom ruffle or whatever, you just hand it to me. Okay?"

"Wait! Hold on for just a minute. I need to make sure I understand this process." Paul waved the instruction sheet at her. "This is the grand plan we're supposed to be following? Sort of like the blueprint for the dress?"

Lenore had never thought of patterns as blueprints, but she supposed so. "Yes," she agreed as she flipped open the direction sheet and pointed out a drawing. "They provide a sample layout, but you don't really need to follow it. See these arrows on each pattern piece?"

Paul nodded.

"Just make sure they point down the straight of grain of the fabric. That's all there is to it."

Paul awkwardly dangled a whisper-weight translucent piece of paper pattern from his large, blunt fingertips as though he were afraid of damaging it. It fluttered from his hand like a trapped butterfly as a wayward air current passed through the drafty basement.

"The straight of what?"

"The straight of grain. Look closely at the material. It's woven from threads on a loom. See the ones that go side to side this way?"

"Yeah."

"That's not it. The threads that go the other way are the straight of grain. Line up the arrows with them when you lay down the pieces. Make sure this one goes on the fold and put the pins in horizontal to the cutting line about every four inches or so. See? Nothing to it. Start with the facings. I'm going to need them next."

The furnace kicked on and the lightweight pattern pieces lying loose on the table began to scatter in earnest.

"Better catch them," Lenore advised around a mouthful of pins.

Paul stepped on several with his large construction boots. That certainly stopped them. "Facings, facings. All right, I've got them."

It would probably be easier to just do the job herself, but Lenore was not about to pass up the opportunity to watch Paul help create a dress. His namesake,

Paul Bunyan, was probably turning over in his grave although it didn't seem to be bothering Paul McDaniels himself in the least. He was obviously one of those rare individuals who didn't feel the need to prove himself. Paul was a man secure in his masculinity.

Lenore paused in her work. Was that even possible?

No, of course not. He was probably just afraid she'd quit if he did. That was it. Lenore turned back to her machine and began stitching the shoulder seams with a hardened heart. She was determined to ignore his mutterings.

Paul only kept her waiting a couple of minutes before handing her the crescent-shaped neck facings. "Here," he grunted. "They're done."

"All I want is the fabric," she told him as she unpinned the pattern pieces and handed the paper and pins back to him. "You can put these into the pin box and stuff the pattern pieces into their envelope."

Lenore removed the last pin from the back facing. Two pieces of fabric fluttered down into her lap. "Uh-oh."

Paul rolled his eyes heavenward and turned to face her. "Uh-oh? What uh-oh?" He couldn't believe the things he was doing tonight all in the name of fatherhood. Parenting was aging him at a very quick rate and Angie darn well better come see him every day in the nursing home he'd undoubtedly be shipped off to sometime early next week—twice on Sundays, or by God, she would hear about it.

"This one was supposed to be cut on the fold, remember? I can't use these."

Disgruntled, Paul snatched them from her hand. "All right, just give them here. Plenty of material

left." He'd made a mistake. So sue him. He was starting to actively hate these giant pink and white hibiscus. "I'll recut it. No problem."

"Hey, it's not my fault you cut it out wrong."

"I never said it was. Now don't talk for a minute.
I've got to concentrate."

In a huff, Lenore swiveled in her seat and stared at
her machine. Men! Who would ever understand them?

Silence reigned in the basement, broken only by the
hum of the sewing machine and Paul's quiet swearing
as he struggled with pattern pieces. It reminded Paul
of an operating room. Every few moments, Lenore
would request a certain piece and Paul would scramble through what he had left in his pile until he found
whatever she'd requested and slap it into her out-
stretched hand. Immediately, she would whip it under the machine and set right back to work.

She was, he thought, a good sport about all this.
And also a darn good seamstress or whatever these
sewing people called themselves. The moment he gave
her the last cut piece, Lenore began handing him partially finished bits and pieces of the dress with in-
structions to press some seam open or turn under a
five-eighth-inch allowance all around the sides of a
pocket and return them to her so she could proceed.
This part he felt more at home with. He'd ironed his
shirts and Angie's things for four years now. Ironing
he could do.

Their primitive version of an assembly line chugged
along. The bits and pieces of hibiscus grew into larger
and larger chunks. Paul was just starting to believe
something they could pass off as a muumuu could
come of the process when Angie and Timmy suddenly appeared in the basement.

Lenore glanced up, startled, and Paul knew she'd been so engrossed in her task she'd completely forgotten the two children. He understood completely. That's how he reacted when he picked up a set of blueprints. The rest of the world would just have to wait its turn until he finally got his nose out of his project.

Lenore blinked. "I guess I thought the two of you had fallen asleep up there."

Hah. She hadn't given them a passing thought since she'd started sewing, Paul thought with a grin.

"We wasn't sleeping. Me an' Angie was talking," Timmy explained.

Voluntarily? Lenore wondered as she thought about the typical disdain Timmy ordinarily displayed when discussing the girls in his third-grade class.

"Weren't," she automatically corrected while mulling over the possibility of Timmy coming down with some virus or flu bug. Should she take his temperature?

"Huh?"

"You *weren't* sleeping. You *were* talking."

"That's what I said."

"Not quite, but never mind. What were you talking about?" She was dying to know what topic of conversation was so engrossing as to overcome a little boy's natural antipathy to girls.

Mere moments later, Lenore thought of all the old sayings and maxims dealing with her current predicament. Curiosity killed the cat. Let sleeping dogs lie. And others she was sure she could come up with given a few more minutes. The point was, she should have learned a long time ago that it never pays to question good fortune. They'd been talking to each other; she should have left it at that. But no, she'd had to ask. And she didn't like the answer.

"But, honey, don't you remember? Dad called and said he wasn't going to be able to take you on the camping trip. So while I think it's neat that Angie's straight hair comes from an Indian great-great-great-grandmother and it's exceptional that she also likes dinosaurs, you two certainly can't go off camping by yourselves."

"Mommm..." His cry was long and drawn out. Pitiful, really. "You're not listening."

Lenore sighed. "Timothy, there are limits to any mother's love. Now while I would gladly be tied to a stake and burned for you, I absolutely draw the line at camping. Angie, darling—" sweet little traitor—how dare you like dinosaurs? "—come here and slip this over your head. Let's see how it's shaping up."

Obediently, Angie came forward. She held her arms over her head and allowed Lenore to settle the dress down over her. "I really do like dinosaurs, Mrs. Pettit," she said through the fabric over her face.

"I'm sure you do, honey," Lenore soothed while she tugged the dress into position.

"Timmy and me are going to study them when we grow up."

"Timmy and I. Okay, I'm done. You look terrific. Put your arms back up so I can get it off."

Angie's skinny little arms rose immediately. "Timmy and I. We're gonna be paleo whatevers when we get growed up."

"Grown up."

"Yeah. We are."

"I thought you were going to be an anthropologist and study Indians," her father interjected from his position at the ironing board, where he was struggling to press the ruffles for the hem of the dress.

"That, too," Angie agreed.

"You're going to be busy," Paul warned.

His daughter was unfazed. "Yeah."

Lenore turned back to her sewing machine, intent on ignoring her son and inserting a zipper.

Like it was possible to ignore an eight-year-old boy. They were budding men after all, and blessed with one-track minds once they got their teeth into something.

"Now, Mom..."

"The answer is no, Tim. It wouldn't be safe for a woman and two children to go into the wilds with nothing but a piece of canvas for protection." Lord, she got the chills just thinking about it. A tent would be nothing but an appetizer for a bear on its way to the main course—her! Nothing doing. "I don't know anything about wilderness survival." And anything west of the Mississippi was wilderness as far as she was concerned. "I'd get us all killed."

"But it wasn't going to be just the three of us. Angie was going to ask her dad to come along, too."

Lenore stared at her son, a bit wild-eyed. She'd been trying to get through an evening in Paul's presence without throwing herself at him, and her son thought he could talk her into two weeks of a similar torture? He'd lost his teeny tiny little eight-year-old mind. "You honestly expect Paul and me—"

"Paul and I," Angie corrected self-righteously.

"No, it's a direct object here," Lenore informed her in a quick aside. "Me is right. I think." Lenore shook her head. "Anyway, you expect us to drop everything and take you two camping just like that? I mean, maybe *I* could, but Paul? Why, he's in the middle of the building season. He can't just take off at the drop of a hat." And thank God for that.

From across the room, Paul took in her consternation. He'd never been much of a camper himself. A couple of YMCA Indian Princess overnights with Angie, that was about it. But really, how hard could it be?

Lenore acted as though there were no roads heading in that direction. They'd have to travel by covered wagon and send the children out for buffalo chips to build a fire at night.

"The Panorama of Homes opens the end of May. I suppose I could take a week off. That would give us almost ten days if we left on a Friday afternoon."

Lenore looked at him, horrified. "You can't mean it."

Paul shrugged. "Why not?" And, in fact, why not? Not only would it help pay back Lenore for what she'd done tonight, but she was one fine-looking woman, and while he had no intention of ever remarrying—it hurt too bad when you lost somebody you'd loved as much as he'd loved Amanda—just lately he could see his way clear to a little hand holding, a little cuddling by the fire while the kids slept peacefully in a tent close by.

"You'd feel safe with Mr. McDaniels there to protect us, wouldn't you?" Her son had sensed the weakness in the parental front and was already moving in for the kill.

Intellectually, it was an interesting notion. Since Paul was as large and as bushy as any bear, Lenore supposed the wildlife out there might mistake him as kin and thus leave them alone, but no, this was a disaster in the making. She knew it as surely as she knew her own name. Lenore, ah...

"Timothy, I really don't think—"

"Please, Mom?" She tried not to look at her son's face, knowing she would be unable to stay strong against what she would see there, but her head turned of its own volition. And there they were, limpid blue eyes that pleaded with her.

"Oh, honey..."

"Come on, Lenore. It'll be a new experience for you and the boy, and I don't really mind, if that's what you're worrying about."

Should she tell him that his comfort was low on her list of concerns right then?

"Please, Mrs. Pettit?" Now two pairs of limpid eyes stared at her. Lenore couldn't stand it.

She caved. "All right, all right, we'll do it. Now you two scoot so I can get this thing finished, or Angie will be going to school in her slip."

Oh God, oh God, Lenore thought after they'd left. She couldn't believe it. She was going camping. If the bears didn't get her, Paul probably would. And the worst part was, she was having trouble convincing herself that that would be such a terrible fate.

Lord help her.

Chapter Four

More than an hour passed before Lenore cleared her house of unwanted company. It took another forty-five minutes to get Timmy to hold still long enough to fall asleep. Good thing the end of the school year was closing in, Lenore thought when she was finally able to drag herself off to bed. Timmy would definitely not be functioning at his best tomorrow in class.

She lay in her bed staring at the ceiling, desperate for sleep. Or unconsciousness. Any form of oblivion. At least then she would escape for a few hours from the knowledge of what she'd done.

How could she have agreed to go *camping?* And not at the Granger KOA a couple of miles down the road. Oh, no. That was too civilized. She was going Out West. A place where dinosaurs had roamed free and unimpeded until the earth had gotten tired of being stomped on and heaved up the Rocky Mountains to move those babies on out of there. What kind of rational response to a couple of animals raising a little dust was that?

The Rocky Mountains. They were so—so very Western. Vast. Overstated. Oversize. Over everything.

Like Paul.

And dinosaurs.

Lenore shivered under her covers. Those creatures were the same way. Overdone. You never heard of any of those things being dug up here in nice, civilized, refined Indiana, now did you?

Her head ground into the pillow when she moved it from side to side. A few discreet Indian burial mounds, sure, but nothing so difficult to comprehend as wildlife as big and tall as a three- or four-story house.

Even if there were dinosaurs buried under the ground here, Hoosiers were smart enough to leave well enough alone. Indiana natives—other than Paul and her own son—were mostly like Lenore. They'd seen *Jurassic Park*. They knew what could happen.

Hadn't that movie been shown west of the Mississippi? Lenore wondered. Restlessly, she turned onto her side. And then there was that Mesa Verde place little Angie was so keen on seeing.

Cliff dwellers.

Would someone please explain to her why she should drive three days in a hot, stuffy, claustrophobic car—with Paul—to go see a place where people of apparently limited good judgment had lived? After all, what kind of people would build their homes on the edges of precipices?

What did that say about Lenore, that she was willing to plan her only vacation of the year around see-

ing such a place? With a man built too much like her
former husband to be anything but trouble but whom
she wanted anyway? With two little kids? One that
didn't even belong to her? Camping?

Lenore tried her other side. It wasn't much better.
But eventually, by dint of sheer determination and a
lot of shoulder rolls and neck stretches, she was able
to relax enough to drift off. Unfortunately, when sleep
finally came, it brought no rest with it. She dreamed
of cowboys and Indians who twirled their lassos while
riding dinosaurs—big *Tyrannosaurus rex* types. Mean
mothers. It was bad enough watching them fight each
other, but then both the cowboys and the Indians
caught sight of her little entourage and came after
them.

Lenore screamed and tried to run while she pulled
Timmy after her with one hand and Angie with the
other.

Paul, being a typical male, sauntered casually behind, laughing, while she did all the work.

She woke up sweating and exhausted.

Timmy wandered groggily into the room. He looked
at her through sleep-slitted eyes. "I heard you call,
Mom. Is it time to get up already?"

Lenore was sitting straight up in bed, her heart racing. She glanced at her bedside clock radio. Three
o'clock in the morning, and she was giving herself
palpitations. What was wrong with her? "No," she
said weakly while she fanned her face with her hand.
"I guess not. I must have mistaken the three for a
seven. Go back to bed. I'm sorry I woke you up."

The beauty of small children, she decided then and
there was that they actually accepted inane and im-

plausible excuses like that. Timmy nodded, turned,
and stumbled tiredly out of her bedroom.

Not that he'd had an accident in years, but once a
mother... "You might as well go to the bathroom
since you're up," she called after him.

"'Kay," he agreed and promptly detoured into the
bathroom.

Moments later, Lenore heard the toilet flush, then
his bed creak as he crawled back in. He really was a
great kid. He deserved this trip.

The real issue was what had she ever done to de-
serve it? Lenore wondered if Paul could be bought.

No, she decided. Then she sighed and started over
with the shoulder rolling and neck stretching. Even if
she had the money, she couldn't trust a man to do
things right. She didn't know. Maybe it was easily explained by their lack of exposure to kids since most
men spent their days dealing with adults. But she felt
sure that men simply couldn't understand the trouble
young children could cook up so quickly and effort-
lessly if no one constantly rode herd on them.

Lenore winced and thought she might have pinched
a nerve with that last neck stretch or perhaps she was
simply feeling pained to find she was already thinking
in Western idioms.

She scooched down until she was flat on her back,
then pulled the sheet and blanket up over her shoulders. Squeezing her eyes tightly shut, she was determined to at least fake getting some rest. Maybe she
could fool her body into not feeling like garbage come
morning.

And Lenore knew she needed to start building up
her strength. There was no getting around the fact that
if she sent Timmy off with Paul, he would probably

come back in a wheelchair—or a pine box. No, she would have to go along and keep them all on the straight and narrow.

It was her role in life, her lot. Queen witch.

She rolled onto her side and pulled the blankets over her head. If Paul had gotten his coconut cupcakes made and was blissfully slumbering in his bed, she would just spit.

The cupcakes awaited the morning and their trip to school down on the kitchen countertop. Not exactly a gourmet production, Paul recognized as he lay in bed staring at the ceiling. Lenore would have done a more—a more *refined* job of it, he guessed was the way he would put it.

Lenore was a refined woman.

Paul comforted himself. "Angie doesn't know any different," he muttered into the quiet of the dark room. "And neither does any other first-grade kid. Those cupcakes may look a little crude, but they'll taste just fine. Especially if they close their eyes while they eat them."

Paul bet Lenore would taste just fine, as well. Only he wouldn't close his eyes in the unlikely event such an opportunity arose. He folded his hands behind his head and began thinking about making love to a more genteel sort of woman.

"The only thing ladylike about Amanda was her name."

And that was the truth. Amanda had been earthy. Paul had never had to worry about offending her. "So now how does an oversize lunk like me go about making love to a discriminating kind of woman?" he wondered out loud.

Would she faint if he slipped his tongue into her mouth when he kissed her?

Amanda had loved the feel of his rough whiskers on her body.

But Lenore seemed more prim and proper. Maybe he ought to shave.

Paul removed one hand from behind his head and ran it through his beard in an effort to judge.

Man, he was going nuts. He was feeling like a sixteen-year-old all over again.

Well, he had a house to build, and he supposed he would have to drive Angie and her cupcakes to school, as well. They would never survive the bus trip intact. He needed his sleep. Damn Lenore *and* her refined sensibilities.

Paul drove more nails into drywall the next day than John Henry had driven spikes into rails during his contest with the steam engine. Paul's crew stood in awe of him by five o'clock that night. Paul alone knew his show of strength had actually been a manifestation of weakness.

Working his butt off had been the only way he could think of to keep his mind off Lenore Pettit.

"Good night, Paul," said one crew member as Paul finally dropped his hammer back into its sling in his carpenter's belt.

"See you Monday, Paul," called another.

He acknowledged both with a wave of his hand. Ten minutes later, Paul was alone in an empty house in an empty neighborhood.

He looked around. They'd finished drywalling the entire basement and garage. Joint taping was well underway. The built-in shelves on either side of the living room fireplace were just about done, and the custom-made kitchen cabinets were being delivered on Monday by an Amish cabinetmaker from Nappanee. They would trim out that room on Tuesday.

Things were tight but very much on schedule.

So why was he feeling so antsy?

He knew damn well why. The source of his malcontent had blue eyes and thick brown hair that curled beguilingly around her small face.

The source of his malcontent was Lenore.

He'd left her house around ten-thirty the night before. Paul glanced at his wristwatch. Five-twenty. Frankly, he figured he deserved a medal for holding off calling her this long.

Paul went out to his truck and plugged the phone into the cigarette lighter. He dialed her number.

"Hello?"

"Lenore? This is Paul. Paul McDaniels."

There was a pause, as if she'd forgotten the name. How could she have? He certainly hadn't forgotten hers.

"Yes?" she finally said.

Paul knew then he was nuts to feel relief. She was going to give him nothing but grief. If his body was so determined to jump back into the swing of things without consulting his brain, couldn't it have picked a less difficult woman for starters? "I was calling to set up a time for tomorrow."

"Tomorrow?"

His jaw clenched shut. It took all his strength of will to keep from grinding his teeth together. She was playing dumb. He knew it. And it was a good thing videophones weren't commonly available just yet. Not only was he grubby and dirty from a day of construction work, but now he was beginning to sweat. It wasn't all that hot out, either. "To go shopping for Tim's baseball mitt?" he prodded.

"Oh, that."

"Yeah." He could almost hear the wheels in her tiny brain whirring as she tried to think of a way to wriggle her way out of it. Well, damned if he was going to suffer in this purgatory by himself. She could darn well burn right along beside him. Could Lenore Pettit burn? It was an interesting concept. Just thinking about it did absolutely wicked things to his blood pressure and the lower half of his body.

"Uh, it's really not necessary."

Oh, yes, it was. He needed to spend some time with her, discover her flaws. Maybe then he would be released from this temporary insanity of an obsession he'd formed about her. "I promised the boy. I always keep my word."

Oh, hah. There, on the other end of the phone, Lenore didn't believe a word of it. If Paul always kept his word, he was the first male of her acquaintance to do so.

"How long do you think this will take?" she asked, knowing full well how ungracious she must sound. This was, however, the man who had deprived her of a much needed night of sleep.

Paul looked at the phone in his hand. The woman needed an exact timetable? He eyed the cigarette lighter and debated pulling the phone plug out right there and then. Make a doctor's appointment instead. Surely there was some kind of shot available for whatever ailed him. If not, someone could make a damn fortune inventing one.

He did some quick mental calculations. "Fifty-five minutes."

That surprised her. "Fifty-five minutes? Exactly?"

"It's a ten-minute drive from your place to Indian Ridge Plaza, right?"

"Uh, yes. About that."

"It being Saturday and all, we'll probably have to park far out. Five minutes to walk from the car to the store. I figure about twenty-five minutes to try all the mitts and pick one out, then the walk back to the car, the drive back to your house—fifty-five minutes."

"Oh." What else could you say to such precise calculations? "I see." He'd given his word to her son but had predetermined the absolute minimum amount of time required to spend in her presence to accomplish his goal? Lenore thought she should be insulted. She would have been better off not asking.

"Of course, we could have some lunch before I brought you back. As a treat for the kids, naturally. I expect we'd have to allow about another hour for that. Tell you what," he concluded smoothly. "Why don't I pick you up around nine-forty-five and we'll just make a morning of it?"

Lenore went from being insulted over the brevity of the visit he'd planned to being amazed at his audacity in expecting an entire morning of her time. "Timmy has to be at practice at one-thirty," she warned.

"We'll have him there," Paul assured her.

"Well . . ." She hesitated and was lost.

"Fine. Angie and I will be there at nine-forty-five." And he pulled the plug, pleased with the way he'd pulled the whole thing off.

Lenore was left listening to a dial tone and wondering what she was getting herself into. Talk about overbearing. Talk about manipulative. Why, she was left virtually breathless in his wake. Strictly from indignation, she assured herself as she finally hung up the buzzing telephone.

She was still breathless the following evening. Paul had first stretched fifty-five minutes into a morning and then into the entire day.

And he'd kept them hopping the whole time. An inordinate amount of time had been spent picking out a mitt—at least it had been on sale—which had left them too pressed for time to go back and pick up her car, so they'd grabbed some lunch on the fly and Paul had driven directly to ball practice. After dropping Timmy off, they'd swung back by the mall to sign Angie up for a children's sewing class at the fabric store.

The inevitable happened. She'd picked up the skirt pattern she'd seen Thursday night. Then, while looking for fabric for that, she'd discovered a navy-and-red print cotton blend that would be perfect on someone with Angie's coloring. Naturally *that* entailed finding a cute younger girl's pattern. She'd found three.

All she'd achieved was two more projects to add to the stacks "aging" in her sewing room, and she still wasn't even. The blame belonged squarely on Paul, of course.

Lenore was embarrassed to admit it, but she'd laughed as they'd raced to get back in time to pick up her son. Then the four of them had hung around the empty ball field, and much to Lenore's surprise, she'd found herself playing Running Bases. And *enjoying* it.

After that, the most bizarre thing had happened. Of her own free will—unless Paul had slipped something into her drink at lunch, and she was beginning to suspect as much since this was so totally unlike her—Lenore had volunteered to make dinner for all four of them.

Now was that freaky or what?

And Paul, being a sneaky male, snapped up the offer so quickly her words were practically still hanging in the air. There'd certainly been no time to retract it.

So they'd gone to the grocery store. Paul had commandeered the shopping basket, insisting he would take care of everything since she'd had such a full day. Thoughtfulness? From a man? Lenore watched as Paul picked out all ready-made things that would be easy to heat. He'd paid for it all, too.

Basically, cooking dinner tonight had consisted of watching and waiting for water to come to a boil for the fresh ravioli he'd purchased.

"Smells good," Paul said from just behind her, right before clapping what Lenore guessed was supposed to be a friendly hand on her shoulder.

Lenore staggered a bit and looked up from her careful perusal of the tiny bubbles beginning to form in the pot of water. "I haven't cooked anything yet." Her shoulder burned under his hand. Why, God? Why him? she silently moaned.

Paul took another sniff. "Must be you, then." In the most natural manner in the world, he began to massage her shoulders and rub her back while they stood there together, waiting for water to boil.

And talk about watched pots. Long before anything productive happened in that pot, she would be melted against him. Good thing the kids were in the next room. Heck, her spine was liquefying already. Then, of course, there would be no room for his hands there, what with Lenore's back plastered up against his front. Paul would have to move his arms around to her front where there would be nothing left to massage but her chest. And what protruded from it.

Suddenly overheated, Lenore peered into the pot once more. "There!" she exclaimed a bit desperately.

Instead of letting her go, Paul pulled her closer and gazed over Lenore's shoulder. Now he was so close, she had to shut her eyes and take a steadying breath.

"What? Where?"

Eyes still shut, Lenore pointed to the pot. "The water. It's boiling. See?" His beard whisked against her ear before lightly prickling her cheek. Lenore felt faint. She prayed she wouldn't make a fool of herself as Paul craned his neck farther forward for a dubious look at the pathetic number of bubbles her hand still pointed out.

"You sure that's enough of a boil?"

"Of course I'm sure. I've been boiling water for years. I know boiling water when I see it." Good grief, she sounded like an idiot, even to herself. But heck, she was a desperate woman. "Now, if you'll excuse me, I've got to pull the cellophane off the ravioli packets." Any excuse at all to get away. Anything.

"I'll help," Paul offered.

"No! It's okay. I can do it."

Paul was looking at her very strangely by then, and Lenore could hardly blame him.

"I'm sure you can. There's just no reason for you to do so when I'm right here, ready, willing and able to help." And besides, it was fun watching her squirm. He'd felt her jump when his beard had touched the side of her face. Right then and there, he'd decided against shaving it off.

"Well, of course you can help if you really want to. You can, um, set the table." The kitchen table was only a few feet away, as Lenore's kitchen was on the small side, but hey, in wars of this nature, inches counted.

Reluctantly, Paul let her go. Setting the table was a reasonable request, he supposed, but he didn't like having to move away from her. Lenore, for all her slightness, had felt amazingly good under his hands.

Paul prided himself on never getting so hung up on winning a battle that he lost the war. He had a much larger goal in mind here. And if he pushed now, he might never achieve it. Time to back off. He knew it, but still, it was surprisingly difficult to turn away and retrieve the dishes from the cabinet.

Conversation, per se, did not exist at the dinner table that night. Whatever talking occurred was more along the line of two simultaneously running but separate monologs. Timmy spent a great deal of time extolling the virtues of his new mitt, and Angie filled them in on every detail of the first grade's luau from arriving with her cupcakes at school to Charlie Felstetner's upchucking of the same. Then she rhapsodized at great length over the fabric she and Lenore had purchased that day and how her new dress was going to be the best ever. She solemnly assured Lenore that she would help her every step of the way, which was exactly what Lenore was afraid of.

Still, it was an entertaining meal and Lenore appreciated the children's chatter. It camouflaged her own silence quite nicely, as she couldn't have squeezed a word in edgewise even if she'd wanted to.

But, squeezing a word in was not a problem, for her brain had shut down and her tongue lay there on the bottom of her mouth, paralyzed and useless. Paul was equally silent, and whenever she peeked from under lowered lashes over his way, she intercepted an equally furtive glance of his.

"Yes, Angie, I think red might be your color."

Something was going on here, Lenore decided, trying to think and carry on a conversation with Angie at the same time.

Paul's voice rumbled out. "I agree. That glove you picked was the perfect choice. Your friend James is all wet on this one."

Lenore lifted up a ravioli. Out of the corner of her eye, she saw Paul's gaze drop to her mouth as she popped it in. Oh, yes. Something was definitely going on here. And old Paul was every bit as aware of it as she was herself. Only the kids were oblivious.

She swallowed and Paul's attention switched to her throat. Darn, she would never eat again. Lenore cleared her throat, picked up the serving dish, and extended it to Paul. "More pasta?" she asked.

His eyes never left her face. "No, thanks. I'm fine."

Reluctantly, she set the bowl down. It was going to be extremely difficult to ignore her libido and not do anything stupid here if Paul wasn't going to cooperate even a little bit, she decided a bit crossly.

"Hmm? Well, I'm not exactly sure when we can start on it, sweetheart. Some time soon, though."

Maybe he was out looking for a new mother for Angie.

Lenore's mouth curled down at that. Well, she wasn't looking for two more children to take care of and to her that's what a man was. Another child.

"I suppose we could start right after supper, but what would your daddy and Timmy do?" Lenore laughed when Angie suggested washing the dishes and the pots and pans.

"Thanks a lot," Paul said with a mock glare at his daughter.

"Besides, it's still so nice outside, wouldn't you rather take a walk before bedtime, all four of us together? There's a park just up on the next block." Lenore left the offer hanging temptingly.

Both kids bit immediately, excited by the novelty of playing in the park at dusk.

Lenore was grateful. She needed the fresh air to cool her face.

She had no idea just *how* much she needed it until Paul insisted on cleaning up the kitchen first.

"The four of us can get it done in ten minutes," he predicted.

It was the longest ten minutes of her life. She'd never noticed how cramped her kitchen was. Whereas before it had been compact, intimate and cozy, tonight it was just plain claustrophobic.

Unfortunately, it was a false deep breath of relief she took as they stepped outside into the early evening air. Immediately, Timmy and Angie ran ahead, and Paul slipped an arm over her shoulder in what she guessed was supposed to be a friendly gesture.

Lenore tried not to take it personally. Paul was, after all, a man who enjoyed working with his hands. He was probably one of those tactile people who had to feel everything, and so long as he kept the touching and feeling confined to her shoulders, she guessed she could cope. Maybe.

"This trip west might be a lot of fun," Paul said as they strolled along. "The kids seemed to be enjoying each other's company tonight."

Lenore had to agree. "Timmy had a good time today, I think."

"I agree. And so did Angie."

The wind picked up and Paul pulled Lenore's sweater up closer around her neck. His hand brushed against it. "You have the smoothest skin," he said.

His non sequitur emphasized the fact that relaxing in Paul's presence was a grave error in judgment.

"Ah..."

He brushed the back of two fingers against her neck again, this time deliberately. "Really incredible."

Lenore tipped her head and looked up at him. Another mistake. His eyes, almost all that was visible what with the dusk and all that facial hair, mesmerized her. She continued to stare up into them.

"You want to go with us to church tomorrow?" he asked.

Probably he thought he had her hypnotized. Hah! Not her. Not Lenore Pettit. She could say no. She *would* say no. "Ah..."

He nodded. "Good. We usually go to the nine-thirty service. Angie and I will come by about five or ten after to pick you two up."

And so it went. For five more weeks.

Angie got a new dress out of the blue-and-red-print fabric. Timmy's mitt was well broken in. Paul came to his games. Together, they drove into Chicago and did the Field Museum one time, Science and Industry another. They had fun, laughed, and Lenore made sure she was never alone with Paul. But he always seemed to be watching her without being obvious about it. Lenore figured he was biding his time.

And then—Lenore was never sure how it happened—time was up.

Chapter Five

"You're sure that's tight enough?"

"I'm sure."

"You're positive?"

"I'm positive."

Lenore eyed the newly purchased and installed car-top carrier critically. "I don't know if we should trust those two little straps that came in the box to hold that great big thing to the top of the car."

"It'll be fine," Paul grunted as he gave a cable one last tug. Wasn't that just like a woman to watch the man do all the work while she "supervised"? "But just to be sure," he started, knowing he'd never hear the end of it if the damn thing fell off, "I've added several stretch cables, see?" He pointed to the bungee cords he'd twined around the base of the carrier and the metal supports on top of the car.

She opened her mouth.

Paul held up his hand. "It's fine. The real question is, have you got everything you need packed and in the car? This grand vacation of ours was supposed to start twenty minutes ago. We're already behind schedule."

Okay, so she was running a few minutes late. So sue her. But Lenore was ready then, and she held up her oversize purse to prove it. "I've got the bug repellent, sunscreen and allergy pills right here."

"All the essentials, huh? What I really want to know is, have you got clean underwear and a tooth brush? I refuse to spend ten days with someone who's got grungy teeth and ten-day-old underwear," Paul said as he rearranged luggage in the trunk for the third time. He immediately regretted his words. That was no way to talk to a woman with delicate sensibilities. When would he learn? "Hand me the cooler, will you?" he asked. Maybe she hadn't noticed his putting his size-thirteen feet into his mouth.

Fat chance.

Lenore knew he'd been teasing, but was unused to his brand of humor. She didn't want Paul thinking she was prissy or anything. But not knowing how to respond, she finally just picked up the cooler and handed it over. Lenore was grateful for the small task. She hated feeling superfluous with nothing to do but hover, especially when the whole trip had been her family's idea anyway. "Here you go."

"Thanks." Paul took it, his head still stuck in the trunk. "Get the kids to go to the john and then herd them into the back seat of the car, okay? We may actually be almost ready to get out of here."

Lenore looked at the bags still stacked in her driveway around his feet and wisely decided to keep her mouth shut. She went to round up the kids instead.

So. Here it was. D-day.

"Angie? Timmy? Go to the bathroom. We're leaving now."

"I don't hafta go," her son immediately protested.

Experience had taught Lenore that that was simply a knee-jerk response. "Try," she advised. "We really aren't going to stop for at least two hours."

Where had the past several weeks gone?

They'd slid by in a haze of—she had to admit it—good times.

She remembered Paul stepping in to coach Timmy's baseball game the night the regular coaching father couldn't make it. Paul had been really into it, and Timmy, well, he'd been in heaven.

Then there'd been the nights Lenore had spent trying to convince Angie that when it came to sewing the red dress, Angie was to do as Lenore said, not as she did, especially when it came to holding pins in her mouth.

And who could forget Paul floating them down the Saint Joseph River in a canoe one beautiful Sunday afternoon when the leaves were first starting to unfurl? And the nights when they'd put on a movie for the kids, then sat at the kitchen table with coffee and just talked.

Good times. And if Paul didn't always ask her opinion before setting up some of his excursions, his intentions couldn't be faulted. That counted for something—a lot, didn't it?

"Come on, you two. I'm not kidding. If we're not pulling out of that driveway sometime in the next two minutes I'm afraid Angie's dad is going to skin us all alive."

Angie giggled. "He wouldn't. Not really. I'm the one with the Indian great-great-grandmother, not him."

"I don't know about that," Lenore disagreed thoughtfully as she ushered the two of them out the door. "The fellow I left outside when I came to get you guys looked like a man not to be messed with. I vote we don't put it to the test. Into the car with both of you."

Paul slammed the trunk as they approached the car. He glanced up. "Okay, everybody in." Then he looked at Lenore. "Did you go to the john?"

Oh, for heaven's sake. "Don't worry about me or my kidneys. We're both fine."

"I'm not stopping for two hours," he warned. He'd traveled with women before. "I mean it."

Lenore slid into the front passenger seat, not deigning to reply. He and Angie had obviously not done a lot of long-distance traveling together. It was six o'clock on a Friday evening, and even though Lenore had fed them all an inelegant but satisfying dinner, she would bet her last traveler's check it wouldn't be more than thirty to forty minutes before Timmy and Angie would decide they were both starving to death and/or needed a pit stop.

Paul had packed the cooler in the trunk. They would be stopping, all right, if for no other reason than to get to the food.

Paul climbed in beside her and started the car.

"Are you sure that trailer hitch you had put on for the pop-up trailer-tent thing you borrowed is going to hold?"

"I'm sure."

"But if the hitch isn't centered on that ball just right—"

"I checked it twice." Paul pulled slowly out of Lenore's sloping driveway and grimaced at the sound of grating metal as the hitch scraped bottom before leveling out when it hit the street. "I'm sure," he restated firmly before Lenore could say anything about that.

They drove into the setting sun for almost half an hour before it began.

"Are we almost there?" Timmy asked his mother.

"Sweethearts, we haven't even left the state of Indiana yet. Ask me in another day and a half."

"Oh, man," her son moaned. "I thought you were kidding."

"Nope." There were certain things one didn't fool around about. Long car trips taken with young children ranked high on that list. Add having to sit next to a masculine magnet for the duration, and already it was proving to be no joking matter. Her fingers were itching to smooth down the wild red cowlick that had sprung up on the back of Paul's head when he'd been fighting with the suitcases in the trunk.

Stop it, she silently admonished them. *Just behave yourself. You could get us all killed.* To say nothing of what kind of conclusions the children might draw should she start getting physically familiar with Paul.

"I know," Lenore said. "Angie, why don't you and Timmy look out your windows for a while? You can play the alphabet game. I bet by the time you've found a word beginning with everything from *A* to *Z,* it will almost be time to stop for a break."

"Oh, man, that's such a dumb game, Mom," Timmy moaned. "Last time it took twenty minutes to find a *J* and *Z* was impossible."

"Do it anyway," Lenore advised in a tone that did not invite any further discussion. Between fighting to keep her hands to herself while she rode next to Paul, and the children already starting to whine, there were definite signs of a tension headache creeping up behind her eyes.

A was no problem. *B* proved to be a stumbling block.

"I got it first," Angie crowed. "Look, there's a *B*. *B* for bus."

"That was on *my* side," Tim protested indignantly. "Angie's cheating, Mom. She's looking out *my* window."

"You tired yet?" Lenore asked Paul. "Want me to take over?"

Paul shot her a puzzled glance before turning his attention back to the highway. "No, why? Am I driving funny?"

"No," Lenore said with a shrug of her shoulders. "I just figured if I had the steering wheel to wrap my hands around, my son's neck wouldn't present quite such a temptation."

Paul grinned. "Try not to let it get to you," he advised. "It's the only way we'll make it through the next few days."

"I know," Lenore said with a sigh and couldn't help feeling a sense of kinship with Paul, the only other adult in the car. The bonds were shifting, changing from Paul and Angie, Lenore and Timmy to Paul and Lenore, Timmy and Angie—the adults a team presenting a united front to the children. It felt odd, but right.

"Mom—"

"Timothy James, what do you want me to do? Poke out her eyes?"

No matter how the idea might appeal, Lenore hadn't raised any fool. Timmy knew better than to out and out agree to that, which only left coming in the back door. "But Angie *cheated* and—"

"Did not."

"Did, too."

"Not, and your leg is over on my half of the seat," Angie complained.

"Is not."

"Is, too."

"All right, all right. Right after we poke Angie's eyes out, we'll chop off Timmy's leg, okay? Now both of you stop arguing right this second."

"But—"

"I mean it."

Paul pulled into the next rest area.

A day and a half later, as promised, the plains ended and the Rocky Mountains jutted straight up in front of them with little or no transition between the two.

"Okay," Paul announced around two o'clock in the afternoon. "We're officially *there*. We'll be rolling into Silver Springs any second now. I vote we do Pikes Peak, then find a campground."

He'd been driving one-handed the last hour and a half. Lenore knew—she'd been counting the minutes since he'd stretched his right hand along the top of the front seat. His fingers had been playing in her hair off and on the whole time. She was sure it was an absent-minded gesture on his part, but still, that, and the increasing altitude had her knuckles white and her nails clenched into her palm.

"How does that sound to the rest of you?"

Paul ruffled her hair then and Lenore thought her nails would go right through to the other side of her hand. She had not been raised in a physical family, the way Paul evidently had. Lenore wasn't used to it. All this casual touching stuff seemed far from casual to her. It had the twitch she'd been developing since meeting Paul coming along nicely and evidently there was this direct connection between the ends of her hair and the junction of her thighs and—well, a lady didn't discuss things like that.

All in all, Lenore was in no condition to tackle driving straight up one of these mountains. There was a lot more to these mountains than she'd anticipated when she'd thought of them in the abstract, back in the relative safety of her living room in Indiana. "Pikes Peak?" she squeaked. Lenore was a flatland Midwesterner. She needed time to adjust her thinking, especially as it became rapidly obvious just exactly how off base her original perceptions had been. These were no oversize Indiana hills.

In fact, when she thought about it, there was a certain logic to her fears. After all, Lenore was a short person. She'd lived her whole life close to the ground. She really shouldn't be surprised she had no head for heights. Meanwhile, however, she had the next week to get through. What to do? "Pikes Peak is around here someplace?"

"Yeah," Paul responded offhandedly, his fingers once again tangled in her hair, driving her to distraction. "Remember me introducing you to John Bu-

chanan the other day? He was out here two years ago
with his family. He told me all about it the other day.
I guess it's a kind of narrow, winding road that spi-
rals up around and around the mountain until you get
to the top. Lots of sheer drops with spectacular views.
The Peak is really up there, too. Over 14,000 feet."

Lenore cleared her throat. Fourteen thousand feet.
She tried to put it into some kind of perspective she
could relate to. Almost three miles. From her house to
the mall, only on the vertical. Any way you sliced it,
it was a long way to fall.

"Would you just look at that sky!" she hastily exclaimed. "No point going today. Not if we're going for
the views. Fourteen thousand feet up, why we'd be
right in the middle of all those clouds. See how overcast it is?" She held her hand out the window. "In
fact, I think it's starting to drizzle."

Paul looked disappointed. "Yeah, I guess you're
right. Well, maybe it'll clear up tomorrow."

"Yeah, maybe." Lenore drew a small breath laden
with relief. She had all night to come up with another
excuse just in case the sun decided to shine tomorrow,
but she was not going up that mountain. Not in this
lifetime.

Lenore seemed tense, Paul thought. He decided to
massage her neck and shoulders a bit. Maybe it would
help. This was her vacation, too, after all, not just his
and the kids. He wanted her to enjoy it. He would
make it his job to make sure they saw and did everything they possibly could. Too bad it was so overcast
today. The drive up Pikes Peak was probably spectacular on a clear day. "Did you see anyplace listed in the
camping guide for this area that looked interesting?"
he asked as he rubbed.

Her hair had been silky, slipping through his fingers like liquid satin. Now that he'd moved onto her neck and slipped his hand under her collar to knead her shoulders, he found Lenore's skin to be smooth, soft yet supple beneath his touch. Basically, he was driving himself crazy in a misguided effort to be kind. When had he gotten into self-abuse? he wondered, for his touching her certainly fell into that category. He'd been working on softening her up, but so far she'd shown no return interest, which meant he'd have to be patient. It was killing him.

With a long-suffering, silent sigh, Paul followed Lenore's direction to a campground. They drove through it before registering.

"Kind of crowded, don't you think?" he asked as they passed through the cramped, filled tent sites.

Lenore looked around her. She rather liked the idea of crowded. Wild animals were people shy, right? There seemed to be an awful lot of campers here. Numbers of families, she observed. Young children raced down the roadway, yelling at the top of their little lungs. Parents disciplined them at top voice so as to be heard from a distance. All those bodies might make for a bit of claustrophobia, Lenore reasoned, but it was better than Timmy or Angie being carried off by a coyote.

"This place is stupid. I don't see a pool."

"I thought you said we were there. Can't we get out of the car now?"

Maybe not.

"Stop at the office," she directed Paul decisively. "We're only staying overnight. It'll be fine here."

Paul frowned as he glanced around one last time. Lenore and the children deserved better than this.

"No," he countered just as firmly. "The sites are too cramped and too close together. There must be something else in the book." He pulled over to the side of the road. Then he took the campground guide out of Lenore's lap and perused it himself. He found another listing for a rancher outside of Silver Springs who rented space to campers during the season. On the map, it appeared to be fairly close, too.

But he'd forgotten to allow for the mountains in the way between here and there. It was an hour and a half of switchbacking before they pulled off the main road. And there was not another camper in sight when they got there. Not one.

"You sure this is the right place?" she asked nervously as they drove down the empty clearing.

"Same name as in the book and right where it's supposed to be. This be the place," Paul responded laconically.

The car and trailer bumped along the unpaved road for five full minutes before they saw anything. "Oh, look," Lenore said gratefully. "There's a house way back there."

Paul headed for it. "Now *this* is what we came west for," Paul said appreciatively. "There's room here for the kids to run around and the scenery is dynamite," he said.

Wrong, Lenore thought. Pretty scenery would have been a picture in a coffee-table book or a *National Geographic* special on television. Pretty became something else when you found yourself physically out there in the middle of it. Then dynamite scenery became wild-looking, primitive, empty, desolate and downright scary and she was not staying here. Paul would simply have to take them back into Silver Springs proper.

The camp's owner cornered them before Lenore had him properly convinced, however. "It's fifteen dollars a night. There's a small shower house over there," said the genuine-looking cowboy in his boots and Stetson as he pointed. "Water pump. Wood for a fire stacked there, three dollars a bundle, watch the embers. Been kinda dry lately. Anything else, I'll be up at the house all night. Just knock."

Paul thanked the man and reached for his wallet. "Would you like a campfire tonight?" he asked Lenore. Finally, his fantasy was about to come to life. Let Angie and Tim toast a few marshmallows and get them settled into the camper, then it would be just him and Lenore, alone, gazing into a glowing fire. He would slide his arm around her and she wouldn't start, as he'd been practicing touching her and getting her used to it without her even knowing. He knew enough to plan ahead in circumstances like this because he was slick and sly.

Lenore's mouth dropped open. Build a fire? Was he kidding? Not when this cowboy person had intimated that the surrounding countryside was dry and should be considered as so much tinder. She wasn't going to be responsible for burning out the entire state of Colorado. "No, thanks," she said quickly. "I think I'll turn in early tonight. Read for a while."

Paul handed over eighteen dollars. "I'll help myself to a bundle of wood," he told the man. "Just a small fire," he said placatingly to Lenore. "Our vacation is officially starting now, and it's not really camping if you don't have a campfire." Besides, he wasn't giving up that easily. "It's been a long drive and the kids will enjoy it." Appealing to their mothering instincts always worked.

"Y'all have a good stay," their host directed. "Got the place to yourselves. Plenty of elbow room for you and the kids."

And then some, Lenore thought in despair as she went to help Paul pop up the camper. When this vacation was over, she would go home to cramped, crowded, *peopled* South Bend and appreciate it in a way she never had before. It might not be a Chicago or New York, but it had three universities going for it as well as a couple of colleges, and she now realized it was an underappreciated hub of intellectualism and civilization. Everything was relative after all.

Something moved in the grass she waded through and Lenore froze, then slowly circled around the rippling straw. Rattlesnakes lived out here, didn't they? Oh, God, give her an earwig crawling out of the potted philodendron in her family room anytime. In fact, she would be willing to kiss the next one she saw. Well, maybe.

Paul set the camper's braces and detached the car before cranking the top of the tent up and dropping the sides out. Lenore never flagged, working next to him until it was all up and operational. The local vermin would have a hard time finding a moving target, she told herself.

Lenore was a trooper, Paul decided as they worked together. He renewed his pledge to make this vacation as enjoyable as possible for her.

"Can you turn on the propane tank?" she asked him. "I'll heat up some soup for dinner."

"Sure." After they ate, he would take them all for a walk, work out some of the kinks and wear the kids out a little. He would have them pick up sticks while they were out. They could still toast marshmallows over the fire even if he didn't end up cuddling with Lenore. Paul would make sure they had memories of this camping trip.

"Angie, come set the table. Timmy, get the milk out of the cooler and pour some cups while I open the box of soda crackers. Come on now. Dinner's almost ready."

He took a deep breath. God, the air smelled great out here. Feeling good about life in general, he went to open the crackers and help Lenore serve the canned soup.

An hour later, Lenore stepped carefully through the grass. Heaven only knew what was hiding down there. She turned around and looked back. The camper was barely visible in the distance. Paul was going to get them lost, she just knew it. "Maybe we should turn around now," she suggested hopefully.

"Nah." Paul immediately put the kibosh on that idea. "I want to get as far as that bluff. See what we can see. Isn't this great, Angie? This trip was a terrific idea, Tim. A man can really breathe out here."

Lenore plodded grimly in the wake of the dementedly grinning threesome. She risked a glance up from searching the grass for wildlife to look quickly around her. They were surrounded by nothing but plant life and vegetation. Breathe too deeply, she wanted to tell Paul, and you'd probably get nothing but a good asthma attack for your efforts with all the pollen floating in the air around here. No doubt about it. They were all going to die.

"There's a big long stick, Angie," Paul said. "Go get it. You can use it for a walking stick now and for marshmallows when we get back."

"Wait!" Lenore called. "What kind of wood is it?"

Paul looked at her, surprised. "I haven't got a clue. What difference does it make?"

"I read somewhere that you have to be careful. If it's poison sumac or something like that, you can make herself sick or even die if you impale food on it to cook it and then eat whatever it was."

"Well then, you look at the stick and see if it's safe," Paul said reasonably and gestured for Angie to hand it to her.

"Me? I only know maples and oaks and that's only if they still have some leaves attached. That thing's as bare as a bone. I have no idea what it is."

Paul rolled his eyes. "Then what do you suggest we do?"

Lenore shrugged. She'd pointed out the difficulty. It was somebody else's responsibility to do something about it as far as she was concerned. "Maybe we could open up some metal hangers and use those?" she offered tentatively.

"This is ridiculous," Paul declared. "We don't have any hangers with us, and even if we did, heat travels up metal very quickly. They'd get too hot to handle in nothing flat. Angie, get the stick. I'll eat the first marshmallow. If I don't die, then the rest of you can use it."

Well, she was using a long-handled fork. She wasn't going to flirt with danger.

By the miraculous grace of God, they found their way back, and at nine o'clock, after Lenore had drowned the campfire with two buckets of water just to make sure it was out, she was still waiting for someone to keel over. In fact, she almost wished Paul would, except that then she would be left alone out here with two small children.

"Bedtime," she announced. For once today, Paul didn't contradict her.

"You heard the lady," he said. "Get your pajamas, a towel and soap. I'll walk you to the shower house."

Lenore stayed behind and stirred the damp ashes, checking them carefully for any signs of life. "People who move to the country to get away from the noise of the city are victims of a cruel and nasty joke," she muttered as she peered fearfully into the darkness crowding in from all sides. "This is the loudest quiet I've ever heard."

It was the strangest sensation to feel so alone and yet know you were surrounded by living things. She could hear the equivalent of an entire stringed orchestra as crickets played stereophonically all around her. Several owls hooted eerily while a whole host of other unidentified creatures were going bump in the night. She watched three points of light bounce their way back from the shower house and went into the trailer herself.

"Okay, everybody into their beds."

There was a brief, mad scramble.

"Daddy, will you read to us?"

"Sure, pumpkin, but just a short story. Big day planned tomorrow."

Lenore didn't even want to think about it. But no matter how upset she was with Paul for constantly overruling her better judgment during the day, Lenore would always treasure this picture of big, gruff

Paul McDaniels hunched over in the too-small trailer, reading a bedtime story to their two children by the light of a propane lantern.

When all was quiet, she softly asked, "Paul, do you want to sit outside for a bit? It's a beautiful night." She wanted to relax for a while before she tried to sleep, but no way was she going out there by herself.

"Hmm? Oh, sure. These two are down for the count. They won't miss us."

"We'll only be a few feet away anyway."

"Right."

They stepped out into the night and made their way over to the drowned campfire ring. Paul sat with his back against a large boulder and reached up to pull Lenore down in front of him. "Sit," he said. "I'll be your back support. You'll be more comfortable."

It all seemed so natural with him. She should feel awkward, ill at ease. She was practically sitting in the man's lap, for heaven's sake. But she felt entirely different instead. Comfortable. Warm. Protected. Things she'd once expected to feel with her first husband but no longer looked for. Amazing.

"Paul, you've been a real brick about this trip," she told him, meaning it. "I couldn't have done it without you."

"You could have," he said matter-of-factly. "But I'm glad you didn't. It's safer for you this way, and Angie and I get in on all the fun."

Lenore delicately cleared her throat. "You and Angie—have you been by yourselves, um, long?"

"Four years," Paul answered quietly and waited for the ache to come. When it didn't, he realized he was finally at peace with what had happened that night. "It's been four years since Amanda died."

"How did she die?" Lenore asked, for the first time finding herself genuinely curious about the man himself. To be honest, it was more scary wanting to delve deeper than merely accepting his current usefulness in her and Timmy's lives.

Paul's hands moved restlessly on her shoulders. "It was a car accident. A little sports car chock-full of high school boys hot-rodding around the neighborhood. The kid behind the wheel was showing off. He'd just gotten his license two months before. He lost control on a curve and spun out right as Amanda came around it from the other direction. She was killed instantly."

Lenore was truly horrified. "How awful!"

Paul shrugged and absently began rubbing the spot where her shoulder blades met in her back.

How did he know it was always tender there?

"My cousin was the same age when she died last spring. Breast cancer. It took over two years to do its dirty work. Amanda never felt a thing. I'm grateful for that."

"But you never got to say goodbye."

"It's more important that she didn't hurt," Paul insisted, massaging a little harder, as though trying to rub out the memories.

Lenore let it go. She doubted Paul would ever admit that he'd had needs back then anyway. He'd probably had to bury them for his daughter's sake. Besides, she was going to melt into a puddle of butter in another minute herself, Lenore thought as she leaned slightly forward to give him better access. But what a sad story. Lenore felt a stab of sorrow for the unknown Amanda and the man she had come to know. They sat in silence for several minutes.

"How about you?" Paul finally asked, sounding almost gruff. "How long have you been on your own?"

"The same. Four years."

"What happened?"

"Richard didn't want a wife. He was looking for a substitute mother. I tried to make it work for five years, but he refused to go to counseling or even to consider that there might be something wrong with our relationship. In the end, I had to cut my losses and move on while I still had my sanity."

"Rough."

"It was for a while, but Timmy and I, we're doing okay now."

"I can see that."

Silence.

"The only thing I haven't been able to get a handle on is the loneliness," Lenore finally offered thoughtfully.

"Yeah?"

"Yeah. I was lonely all during my marriage, and, well, I guess I still am. I love my son dearly, of course, but that's not the kind of companionship I'm talking about, you know?"

"Yeah," Paul agreed. "I know what you mean."

Lenore didn't say it, but she acknowledged it privately. She hadn't been lonely during the past month. Not since Paul had walked into her life. Was it truly possible for a man to be both companion and lover? Just when she thought she knew the answer was no, Paul had her wondering again.

She sat with him in the intimacy of the dark pondering the question, oddly comfortable with the silence between them.

Eventually, he stirred. "You ready to go back in?"

"Yes," she said and rose.

Paul led her over to the camper door. His hand was on the handle when he turned and lifted her chin with his other hand so that Lenore was looking up at him instead of carefully perusing the ground. "Good night," he said and kissed her softly.

On that beautiful warm June evening, Lenore went to bed with goose bumps.

Chapter Six

Lenore opened her eyes and lay there in the dark. Something had awakened her. What?

"Oh, my God!" She clamped her hand over her mouth to stifle any further involuntary noise she might make and sat straight up. Her heart pounded against her ribs, doing its best to escape the confines of her chest.

"Paul," she whispered urgently, trying to wake him without alerting whoever and whatever lurked outside. "Don't panic," she ordered herself. "Predators sense panic. It's a signal for them to move in for the kill." And she was the kill. Oh God, oh God, oh God. "Paul!"

At long last, Lenore heard him roll over. Thank the Lord!

"What?" Paul answered sleepily.

"Shh."

"Okay, fine." That was a woman for you. Wake you up to tell you to be quiet. Maybe he'd been snoring. He'd never had any complaints before, but one never knew. He pulled his sleeping bag back up over an exposed shoulder and tucked his head under the pillow.

Lenore couldn't see him, but she could hear him getting ready to go back to sleep. She panicked again. "Paul, wake up!"

Groggily, he raised his head once more. "I already said *what* before," he reminded her. "You told me to be quiet."

"Shush . . ."

"See?"

"There's something outside the camper," Lenore whispered in an effort not to draw the thing's attention to them. Did canvas walls do anything to block the smell of humans, or was that too much to hope for? She could hear whatever it was snuffling around outside.

"What?"

"I don't know what. Something big, though."

They listened as they lay there in the dark. There was an awful lot of heavy clomping going on next to their tent trailer.

"I think there's more than one," Paul offered helpfully.

"Oh God, I cooked the soup on the range here in the camper," Lenore remembered, feeling on the verge of hysteria. "You're not supposed to sleep in the same place where you prepared food, are you? It's a family of bears, I know it is. They've followed the scent of that chicken vegetable soup and it brought them right here. The soup's gone and now they'll have us for dinner instead.''

Life was so unfair. One little mistake and, *tough luck, sister,* you're bear bait. She could just weep when she thought of those two beautiful little children sleeping blissfully through their last moments on this earth, appetizers for some horrendous carnivore with six-inch eyeteeth.

To say nothing of herself. When she thought about what she'd spent on cute shorts outfits to wear on this trip so she could impress Paul, outfits somebody else—Goldilocks, the way her luck was running— would wear now... "We've got to do something.''

"Like what?'' came Paul's laconic reply.

Darned if she knew.

The car had metal sides. Even a bear would have trouble charging through that, Lenore thought.

But there was no way to get to it, not without waving a white flag from the doorway and asking the Ursidae clan outside to be good sports and offer them free passage.

Lenore had approved of the camper when Paul had suggested it. It was up on wheels. They weren't sleeping on the ground. The bottom third was metal, which was fine. It was the top two-thirds that concerned her now. That part was stitched-up canvas and cowardly canvas at that. Look at it shiver just above her toes on the opposite wall as some animal did nothing more than snuffle up against it. In any kind of contest with a bear, she was sure it would give up without a whimper.

Desperately, she thought. There was no place to hide, crawl into or under in the efficiently organized trailer. Every inch of it had been utilized.

"How deep is a bear's heart in its chest?" she asked.

"Oh, for God's sake," came Paul's disgruntled response and she knew he'd been about to fall back asleep. How could he? They were all about to die. Didn't he at least want to slip his boots onto his feet so he could die with them on? What kind of man was he?

"Well," she began defensively, "I was just remembering that we didn't pack anything that would pass as a butcher knife. Not even a steak knife. All we've got are plastic dinner knives. I didn't know if they were long enough to do the job, that's all." There. It made perfect logical sense to her, so he could just put that in his pipe and smoke it.

Paul had no idea what was out there and he wasn't about to open the door and ask. If it was a bear and it had the poor manners to come through the tent sides and try for a late-night snack, he'd do everything in his power to protect what he was coming to think of as his nontraditional but still real little family. But quite frankly, he'd rather use his bare hands and try to strangle the thing than rely on a plastic picnic knife for much protection. "The tips are too blunt. The plastic would snap before you punctured a hide that thick. Besides, if you try anything at such close range, you'll be dead anyway."

"Oh."

Neither of them spoke for a moment, but it was far from quiet. The voracious wild beasties just outside their camper made no attempt to hide their presence as they surrounded the trailer in preparation for the kill. Lenore figured they hoped to spook the tent's occupants into making a wild run for it, thereby adding a little spice in the form of a chase to what must seem like an almost-too-easy sporting opportunity.

"Listen, Lenore," Paul finally said. "I am a virtual role-model paragon from seven o'clock in the morning until nine o'clock at night. But it's two in the morning. I'm off duty. Unless you can think of something constructive for me to do, I'm going back to sleep."

Lenore snapped her fingers—quietly. "Too bad we didn't pack any pepper spray. I bet that would slow whatever that is down."

She could almost *feel* Paul's shrug in the dark. "Oh, well," he whispered, "live and learn."

Or not, as the case may be. Lenore could hear him burrowing down into his sleeping bag and slapping the pillow back over his head and was absolutely furious. What kind of response to impending disaster was that? The least he could do was stay awake and keep watch with her. Considering these were the last moments of their lives, was that asking too much?

Evidently so, Lenore thought moments later when Paul's light snores once more filled their confined sleep area.

It was almost a disappointment when, after an hours-long vigil, the sun finally rose and they were still alive. Whatever had been out there had shuffled off into the predawn darkness, evidently satisfied with having terrorized her. Lenore only hoped they'd left some kind of sign, like humongous teeth marks in the side of the camper to show the mortal danger they'd been in. She would take great personal delight in pointing them out and self-righteously saying, *See, told you so.* Immature response, she recognized, but fulfilling.

But alas, it was not to be.

"Those are horse prints."

"*Horse* prints?"

Paul rose from his examination of the ground outside the trailer and brushed his hands off on his jeans. He looked well rested and fresh. Lenore hated him for it; she had hardly slept at all. She felt lackluster, out of sorts and just plain cranky.

"You're sure?"

"Look for yourself," he invited, gesturing to the surrounding trampled grass. "What else could it have been?"

Lenore studied the U-shaped prints covering the area. What else indeed? "I suppose the horses belong to the guy who runs this sad excuse for a campground," she admitted grudgingly. "He could have warned us they ran loose at night."

"Probably just didn't think of it," Paul offered consolingly.

"Probably." At least Paul hadn't said told you so the way she would have had they found signs of a bear or cougar outside their door this sunshiny morning. It was small comfort.

"Well," she said, sighing. "I guess I'll start breakfast."

"Yeah. I'll rouse the kids. We've got a lot to do today." The rancher who ran the campground had told him about Cripple Creek, an old gold rush mining town not too far away—by Western standards—that Paul thought the kids and Lenore would love.

"I've got a tube of refrigerator sweet rolls in the cooler," Lenore told him as she opened the door to the camper.

"How are you going to cook them?" Paul asked. "We've only got a range top, no oven."

"I'm going to make an oven," Lenore informed him
smugly.

"Lenore—"

"No, I'm serious."

That's what he was afraid of. The woman was going to build her own oven. Terrific. Paul decided then
and there to talk to the shrink who lived two doors
down as soon as he got back home. Ordinarily, he
avoided the guy like the plague. After all, the man
couldn't understand women all that well since his own
wife had taken off on him, tired, Paul guessed, of
Rodney psychoanalyzing everything from the fact that
she liked to wear navy blue to her relationship with his
mother.

His two children were horrible little monsters who
needed some firm parameters set instead of Daddy
being quite so concerned over the slim possibility of
damaging those particular little psyches. But Paul
figured Rodney might well be his last hope. By the
time this trip was over, he would be desperate to understand how he'd reached such a low in his life that
he could be in, so far, a month-long painful state of
constant semiarousal. He'd been brought to his knees
by a woman who was a complete flake.

First it was killer horses. For God's sake, *horses* that
were going to eat them alive. And now she was going
to build her own oven for a couple of lousy refrigerator rolls. "Just give them some cereal," he advised.
"It's a lot simpler."

"I'm sure it would be. But this will be so much more
fun." Lenore had done some research once she'd accepted the inevitability of taking this trip. She had a
number of things she wanted to try out that would be
something different for the two children to experience

and have the added benefit of impressing Paul with her cleverness. "You know Barb in your office?"

Paul looked at his wristwatch. Seven o'clock. Time was a-wasting here. Maybe he should get the cereal out himself. "Yeah?"

"Well, Barb was a Scout leader for a long time when her kids were little. She gave me some great ideas for cooking out. We found this box oven thing in her garage."

Curiosity got the better of him. He would do well to remember what it had done to the proverbial cat. Still, he had to ask. "That liquor box wrapped up in a million layers of tinfoil you insisted on bringing along?"

"Yes," she agreed eagerly. "I can hardly wait to try it." Lenore knelt and began searching the small storage area under Paul's bed that he'd converted back into a bench for the daytime. "Barb says it really works. She says to light the charcoal, and once it's white, each briquette is equal to fifty degrees."

"Where the heck is that thing?" Lenore crawled on her hands and knees over to the next storage area under what had been her bed, but with the mattress removed and the supports raised, was now a small table with two side benches.

Paul reached into the cooler and retrieved the milk. "Lenore—"

"I can hardly wait to try this. I never got to be a Scout, you know."

Paul pulled the cereal box out of the storage area Lenore had just abandoned. He set it on the table. "No, I didn't, but, Lenore—"

"My mother said it was a paramilitary organization and refused to let me join, but all my friends had a blast. I was always so jealous."

Paul put bowls and spoons on the table over Lenore's head. They really needed to get moving. The campground master, or whatever you called the people who ran these things—king of the grounds, whatever—had assured Paul there was a Laundromat in Cripple Creek. They had three days of laundry to take care of. Once she thought about it, Lenore would appreciate clean clothes more than a chance to rectify childhood wrongs, he was sure. And this gave her an opportunity to get waited on a little bit. She was a single parent; she ought to appreciate somebody else taking care of getting a meal on the table. And he didn't mind, not really. "Lenore—"

"Well, here's the charcoal at least. Now all I need is the lighter fluid, the matches, that little disposable tin pan I brought to put the charcoal in in the bottom of the oven and the oven. Where *is* that thing?"

"Breakfast is ready," Paul announced calmly above her.

She banged her head on the bottom of the table. "What?"

Paul steadied the cereal box to keep it from toppling over and set a bunch of bananas down next to the gallon jug of milk. "Everything's all taken care of. Come on out from underneath there and eat." He'd hesitated to disturb her searching. It certainly had provided a provocative view of her rear. If the children weren't running around someplace nearby he'd— Paul sighed. The children *were* around and the day was moving on without them. Another time. Another time *soon*.

Lenore hastily backed out from under the table. "What do you mean, 'breakfast is ready'?"

Paul gestured at the small table. "Look. Everything's taken care of. All you have to do is sit down and eat. How's that for service?"

Lenore stared at the table in dismay. "But I—"

"Angie! Tim!" Paul bellowed out the camper door, pleased with himself. He was really making an effort to do more than his fair share, he decided. "Come eat!"

"Okay, Dad. We're coming."

Still stunned, Lenore allowed herself to be pushed into the booth. Paul slid in beside her when it would have made much better sense for one big person and one little one to each take a side, but she was giving up on understanding men in general. She'd thought it was just Richard she'd been unable to fathom, but if anything, this camping trip was teaching her that Mother Nature had failed to provide her with the key to the lock of the species in general.

Paul filled her cereal bowl way too high before overloading his own. He was only slightly less heavy-handed with the children.

"Thanks."

Paul grinned at her, pleased with his thoughtfulness. It had been a long time. "You're welcome."

Lenore stared at that mouth. He really had a beautiful smile. Handsome, she corrected herself. There was nothing pretty about his mouth or any other part of Paul's body. He was all male and Lenore was as aware of Paul's masculinity as she'd been of the wild beasts outside the camper last night.

Grudgingly, she admitted to herself there would be other opportunities to use the box oven. Paul's proximity, his leg pressed against hers under the table and his one arm slung carelessly across the back of her seat as he ate with the other had a lot to do with the dissipation of her temper. The heat of his arm and his leg burned the anger right out of her.

"So," Paul began conversationally, "I was thinking that when we went down to the sand dunes and Mesa Verde, we'd only be a hop, skip and a jump from the Grand Canyon."

Lenore blanched. Nobody had said anything to her about any Grand Canyon. She'd heard from friends who had been there that the trail down was extremely narrow and that the donkeys, the *donkeys,* for God's sake, got the right of way. Pedestrian traffic had to pass on the outside edge. People probably fell into the canyon all the time. You just didn't hear about it because it was such a long way down the bodies decomposed and scattered to the four winds before they could hit bottom.

Now, how could she phrase her refusal without scaring the children? Lenore tried to think. Paul's arm and leg made it difficult. He was much too quick for her.

"But yesterday, the fellow here mentioned this Phantom Canyon that's someplace around here. He said it was every bit as good, even if it was on a smaller scale than the Grand Canyon, and if we did that one, there'd be no need to bother with the other. What do you all think?" He looked around expectantly.

Lenore's eyes widened as she took in the glowing faces across from her. Well, what else had she expected? The kids were young and naive. They would make terrific adolescents. *Hey, kids, let's all go for a long walk on a short pier.*

"Wow! Can we really do something like that?"

"Oh, Daddy, this is going to be the best vacation ever. I can hardly wait."

Wasn't anyone going to ask her opinion? Lenore thought the idea stank. In fact, she thought—

"Lenore?"

Paul was looking at her. Was she actually going to tell them what she thought now that the opportunity presented itself? They all looked so eager. "Ah...we'll see." It was the typical parental cop-out and she was slightly ashamed of herself, but only slightly. "If there's enough time, we'll think about it." She would make darn sure there wasn't.

"All right." Paul clapped both palms down on the tabletop and pushed himself up. "Finish your cereal, grab your laundry bags, and let's get this road on the show."

"Show on the road," Lenore absently corrected as she hurriedly scooped up the last few bites of cereal. Finished or not, she had a feeling the spoon would be grabbed right out of her hand any second.

"He says it that way on purpose," Angie informed Lenore as she drank the last of her milk right out of the bowl and cleaned her lips with her little pink tongue. "He thinks it's funny." It was the child's universal lament at a parent's pitiful attempt at humor.

Well, the joke had gone clean over Lenore's head. But then, she figured much of this trip would. Lenore sighed and pushed her way out of the booth. "You heard your father. Give me your dishes so I can rinse them out. Timmy, find the laundry detergent, and let's all jump in the car before he leaves without us."

The kids scrambled, and Lenore swished the dishes through a pail of soapy water, feeling more alone than she'd ever felt in her life.

The drive to Cripple Creek really wasn't too bad. The mountains they traveled through were so tightly packed together, it was difficult to tell where one began and the other left off. The road was probably quite high compared to sea level, but there wasn't enough room left between the upthrusting peaks for any of the dramatic scenic drop-offs this area seemed to specialize in. Lenore liked it just fine. They reached Cripple Creek with her nerves pretty much intact.

"Let's take care of the laundry first," Paul suggested as he pulled the car into a parking slot in front of the only Laundromat in town.

"Fine," Lenore agreed.

They took over several machines, fed the beasts a ton of quarters, then sat down to wait.

"You want to take them on a walk or something? I can sit here and watch the clothes," Lenore offered.

"No, no. You go see what there is to see with the kids. I'll wait here," Paul responded, feeling quite noble.

"You folks just visiting for the day?"

Paul turned around to see who had interrupted his discussion with Lenore. It was the guardian of the Laundromat, or whatever you called the head washer and dryer. "Yes," he confirmed. "Tomorrow we head south to see the sand dunes."

The chief launderer nodded his head in understanding. "Thought so. Well, no point all of you sittin' here watching the clothes go 'round and 'round. You can do that anytime, anyplace."

"Right," Paul agreed. "That's just what I was saying."

The man reached behind his counter with one hand, then extended his palm out to them. "Look," he said. In his hand lay six small blue-green stones.

"Is that real turquoise?" Lenore asked.

"You bet it is," the man admitted proudly. "Used to be real plentiful around here. In fact, at one point there was so much of it, they paved the streets using turquoise."

Timmy and Angie crowded closer, impressed. "Is that true?" they demanded.

"Yep. Still some around, as a matter of fact. Found these little guys in the bottom of my machines when I clean them out. Here, you can each have one." He gave each of the children one of the small stones.

They were thrilled.

"Now what you all've got to do is keep your eyes down while you're out walking. Pay special attention by the curbs. Every now and then, somebody who's paying attention to such things'll still find a decent-size one."

"Oh, wow!"

He nodded sagely. "Yep. Why don't you two take your mom or your dad and head over to the train depot? Buy yourself a ticket before they're all sold out for the day."

"Where's the train go?" Lenore asked.

"It's an old narrow gauge that used to bring down the gold ore. Now it takes you up the side of the mountain where you can get a close-up look at some of the old abandoned mines, including the old Bonanza mine." He winked at Paul and Lenore.

Timmy and Angie were suitably impressed. "Bonanza," the boy breathed reverently. "Was it a big strike?"

Lenore smiled at Paul over her son's head. He grinned back. She felt close to him just then. Another one of those times when you could feel their bonds realigning themselves. This made several times now that she and Paul had shared a smile, enjoying their children's behavior and reactions to this trip, just like any normal married couple would. It was a strange sensation.

"You bet. You'll hear all about it on the train trip. Don't forget to look for turquoise on your way there and back."

"We won't. Let's go, Mom."

"Oh, yes, please, Mrs. Pettit. We don't want the tickets to get all bought up."

"Heaven forbid." Lenore looked up into Paul's face. What a great face. "Are you sure this is okay with you?"

He shooed them out the door with another grin that twisted something in the vicinity of her heart. "Go on. Get out of here. Bring me back something to eat."

"You're hungry already?" Lenore asked in surprise.

"Yeah." And he'd have to make do with food for now.

The threesome walked away, and Paul swallowed hard. Bright sunlight turned Lenore's hair to fire as he stared through the plate-glass window separating him from them. Yeah, he was hungry. Starving was more like it. For her, looney as she was.

He smiled to himself when he saw them purposely scuffing their feet, then checking carefully to see if they'd uncovered anything interesting. He turned back to the washing machines. Almost time to transfer the loads.

* * *

Cripple Creek hadn't been too bad, Lenore decided as they drove away around five o'clock that afternoon. Their clothes were clean and neatly folded in a basket in the trunk, which was good. The children had a couple of little bits of turquoise in their pockets. And the train ride had hit just the right happy combination of scary and informative to make all of them content. Quite frankly, the rest of them owed her their lives, not that they would ever admit it. She'd kept that thing on the side of the mountain by dint of sheer concentration and willpower. It wouldn't have dared fall, not with the way she'd prayed the whole time. It had clung to the side of that mountain like a good little train should, and she, for one, was grateful.

"You sure you want to try a different way back?" she asked as they left Cripple Creek behind.

"You saw the map," Paul said as he watched the road in front of him. "This is a lot shorter. I can't think why the guy at the campground told us to go the other way. It's obviously a much longer route."

Spoken like a true born-and-raised Midwesterner.

Following the route they'd traced on the road map and six miles out of Cripple Creek, they drove through Victor, another out-of-the-way and even smaller town currently living on past golden glories. Several long, tortuous miles later, the road turned to dirt.

"Paul, the sign says Proceed At Your Own Risk."

"I see it," he grunted, slowing down even further. "I see it."

"Maybe we should turn back."

"It's already six-thirty. We've been driving for quite a while. That's a lot of backtracking to do and I want to reach the campground before it grows much darker.

We can't have that much farther to go. How bad can it get?''

Call it female intuition, but somehow Lenore just knew they were about to find out.

Chapter Seven

"This isn't so bad," Paul offered some fifteen minutes later.

The road was dirt and it ran through the country-side with a minor detour or two around some low bluffs. "No," Lenore cautiously agreed. "Not too bad." *Yet.*

Twenty minutes after that, Lenore fervently wished Paul had kept his big mouth shut. Somehow, as soon as a comment was made on how well things were go-ing, inevitably all hell broke loose. The dirt road had narrowed to a single car width and was starting to do an imitation of a sidewinder snake in its final death throes. The path they followed was rising, but not as quickly as the bluff to their immediate left. Unfortu-nately, at the same time, the ground on their right was rapidly sinking. They were, quite literally, between a rock and a hard place. Their road had no shoulder, no margin for error. They were in the middle of nowhere, hadn't seen another soul in over an hour, and the sun showed definite signs of fatigue as it inexorably sank lower in the sky.

"What happens if we meet someone coming from the opposite direction?" Lenore asked as they climbed higher still.

Paul had sensed Lenore's growing tension. He sought to reassure her. "There seems to be strategically placed spots wide enough for a car to pull over and let someone by."

"What if we don't happen to be at one of those strategic spots when we meet?"

Paul shrugged far more nonchalantly than he was feeling. It was his role to keep everyone calm. Something told him Lenore was on the verge of getting hysterical enough for both of them. "One of us will have to back up, I guess."

Around all those blind curves? For God knew how far back? Maybe in the dark? "Which one of us?"

"Whoever's got the least distance to go back to a wide spot."

"We'd have no way of knowing which one that would be."

"Quit worrying about it. We haven't met anyone yet, have we?"

She wished he hadn't said that. Paul had slowed to twenty miles an hour. He took the next curve at fifteen and there it was. A tan sedan coming straight for them. "Oh, my God." It was her worst nightmare come to life. The last little niche they'd passed was at least a mile behind them. She would make the children get out of the car while Paul backed up. She would wait with them here so they wouldn't have to witness his death when he misjudged his distances and slipped over the edge into the abyss. She would—

"Look," Paul said, pointing out. "There's a passing spot right there. He's already pulling over to let us by."

Lenore closed her eyes in relief. "Thank you," she whispered in a soft prayer of thanksgiving as Paul inched by the other vehicle and tried not to graze its side while still keeping his right wheels on the road. "That was close," she muttered as they squeaked by.

"But we did it."

This time, she thought. This time, but what about the next? She was too young to die. Although she'd known the time would come when she would meet her Maker, Lenore had it planned for some time in the future. The far distant future. She was definitely not ready for an up-close and personal encounter with the Lord.

Lenore closed her eyes and began making rash promises. If He would just get her out of this mess, she would—

"Would you look at that view down there?"

Her eyes popped open. "What are you doing looking at the view? You're supposed to be driving the car."

"Well, I don't want to miss this. It's absolutely spectacular." In an un-Indiana kind of way, of course. The exposed layers of rocks and the scenic drop were compelling and rich but not fertile or verdant the way Indiana was. Here any greenery was next to nonexistent. The color palette was definitely different in this part of the country but it was no less spectacular with its browns, oranges and rosy rock hues.

Lenore had purposely been keeping her head averted. Now she risked a quick peek. Spectacular? How could he tell? They had climbed so high by this time, the bottom of the canyon—or whatever this godforsaken hole in the ground they were next to was called—was so far down, you'd need binoculars to see anything. "Listen," she said, "you want to see the view? Stop the car and let me drive. Then you can look all you want and I won't say a word. Promise."

"I haven't driven you over the edge yet, have I? Relax, I'm fine."

"Stop looking and I'll be fine, too."

"Daddy, I've got to go to the bathroom."

"I told you to go before we left town, pumpkin."

"I did. That was a long time ago."

"Well, I'm sorry, kiddo, but there isn't any place to pull over here."

No kidding. And here came another car. Oh, help.

"This is amazing," Paul exclaimed.

Lenore would have used a much stronger word.

"Both times we've met an oncoming vehicle, it's been right at a passing spot. Look. They're already pulling in."

Yes, the oncoming car was smart. They were hugging the side of the cliff and leaving the edge of the abyss to Lenore and Paul. Lenore could hardly fault them. Given half a chance, she would have done the same. She scrunched her eyes shut, held her breath, hung on to the edge of her seat for dear life and leaned left. Lenore figured they could use any additional small advantage she could give them to stick to the little ledge some fool had labeled a road.

"You can open your eyes now. We're past them."

Paul knew Lenore was genuinely terrified, but he had

no clue how to help her. For one thing, he didn't understand it. What good was being scared? It wasn't as if it accomplished anything. Why didn't she just relax and enjoy the surrounding beauty? It was so different from Indiana. "You know what I think?"

"What?" It was the only way she'd ever know what a man was thinking. Have them tell her directly. What a fool she'd been last night to think she would ever get anything but ulcers from a relationship with a man.

"I think we found Phantom Canyon all on our own. What else could this be? It's just the way the campground owner described it. A little Grand Canyon."

Lenore considered that. It was a possibility. She was certainly as frightened as she'd anticipated being at the Grand Canyon. "And you know what *I* think?"

"What?"

"Look across the gorge to the other side. No! Never mind. I'll just tell you what's there."

"What?"

"A trail that switches back and forth down the whole face of that side. My guess is that that's where we're headed when we're done scaling this side."

Paul glanced over, looking anyway.

"I told you not to look."

Lenore was right. He could see the faint outline of a road zigzagging down the face of the opposite cliff. That meant they'd yet to reach the halfway point. Paul eyed the sun consideringly. This was not going to be a whole lot of fun in the dark. He would hate to have to go into reverse for any oncoming traffic then.

Well, no point in thinking negatively. It was early June. The days were long. They might have another hour, hour and a half of light. They would make it. Maybe. God, they were high. It was the kind of place that reinforced a person's belief in the Almighty. Take a gander out that window. Talk about the proof of His wonder and glory. It was all around—but mostly beneath them.

"Daddy, I wasn't kidding. I really gotta go."

"Me, too," Timmy declared.

"I'm really sorry, but you're both just going to have to hang on. There isn't even enough room for you to get out and use the side of the road."

And that was the truth, Lenore thought as she glanced around, an act she immediately regretted. They were unbelievably high and unblessed with wings. The dirt path Paul had determinedly followed was barely wide enough to accommodate the car.

No doubt about it, they were all going to die.

"Mom..."

"Think of something to take your mind off it," Lenore advised. "Paul's right. We can't stop here."

"But, Mom..."

"I know. Let's sing a song. What about 'Row, row, row your boat'? We could do it in parts. Or 'Old MacDonald had a farm'?"

"Eei-eei-oh?"

"That's the spirit."

"This is really dumb. I'm just glad Jackie Redding isn't here to see this."

So was Lenore. Tim's friend Jackie Redding was a pain in the whazzoo.

For over an hour, Lenore led the singing while keeping her eyes directed straight ahead of her. Paul got them to the top of the canyon and nearly down the other side before dusk set in. The road was almost level and had just about straightened itself out by the time he had to flick on his headlights. Best of all as far as Lenore was concerned, it had opened back up to two lanes.

Headlights approached them. The occupants of the car gaily waved as they went past.

Lenore was horrified. "I sure hope they're locals who know what they're doing," she said. "It's going to be pitch-dark before they're even halfway through that canyon."

"No point worrying," Paul said. "There's nothing we can do anyway."

If he said that one more time, Lenore promised herself she would do something violent. It brought to mind the horse episode, which in her opinion, did not bear thinking about. Annoying though it was, Lenore tried to take Paul's advice and put the other vehicle out of her mind. It was going to take all her strength to wish her own little foursome home in one piece. *There's no place like home, there's no place like home.*

Lenore had always enjoyed *The Wizard of Oz,* had always empathized with Dorothy's struggles to get home. Well, no more. Dorothy's journey back to Kansas had been a piece of cake compared to what Lenore had been through today. "I've never been so glad to be back anyplace in my life," she told Paul an hour later. The children had gotten to the bathroom before things got embarrassing, and Lenore had served them bologna sandwiches and carrot sticks for supper, not having the energy to try to produce anything fancy. That lousy excuse for a road had finally deposited them back at the campground some forty minutes ago—around eight-thirty—and Lenore had worked like a wild woman getting the children fed and tucked into their beds on opposite sides of the camper so they wouldn't be overtired the next day.

Lenore's nerves were still very much on edge as she swished their utensils through a bucket of hot soapy water.

"Come on," Paul said. "Let's step outside and stretch our legs a bit."

It was a good idea, Lenore decided. She needed to do something to release the tension if she was ever going to sleep. Jumping jacks, run a few miles, have Paul make wild love to her until she was exhausted, something. "Okay."

Not a soul greeted them as they moved out into the night. Theirs was still the only camper on the grounds. Paul draped his arm around Lenore's shoulders and tipped his head back. "Unbelievable," he said. "Just look at that sky. Ever see anything like that before in your whole life?"

Lenore looked up. Millions of stars burned holes in the overhead darkness. It truly was a spectacular view, worthy of the Fourth of July, a sort of black-and-white preview of the upcoming holiday. "You know," she said, "when Richard and I moved from Chicago to Indiana, I couldn't believe the difference in the number of stars you could see. But this, well, you're right. It's unbelievable."

Paul tried to find the Big Dipper. "There are so many stars out tonight, it's hard to identify even the major constellations."

Lenore continued to gaze up. "I see what you mean. Good thing we're not lost."

Paul wasn't so sure about that. He was beginning to suspect he might, in fact, be just that. But not in the way Lenore meant. And he was none too happy about it, but he made a decision to worry about it some other time. Not tonight. Tonight was special. He could feel it.

They stood outside the camper for several minutes in companionable silence. Finally, Paul stirred. He looked over at Lenore. Her upturned face was beautiful in the pale moonlight. "You tired?" he asked. "We could turn in." He made the offer reluctantly. It was so peaceful out under the night sky. He hated to do anything to break the mood of contentment that had settled over them. In the morning, dealing with the children and sight-seeing would do that soon enough, he was sure. For now, though, his sense of rightness could only be improved if Lenore was under him instead of next to him.

Lenore shrugged, unaware of his thoughts. "I'm still too wired to try to sleep," she said. "I think I may spread a blanket on the ground out here for a while and let some of this serenity soak into my bones."

Dipping her head down, she studied the ground by her feet. "You, um, want to stay with me for a little bit?"

Was she kidding? Well, she wouldn't have to ask twice. "You wait here," he directed. "Find a spot where we won't have a lot of rocks under our backs while I get a blanket." Paul paused, one foot inside the camper door. "You want a pillow, too?" He didn't wait for her response. "I'll get one, just in case."

My goodness, for a large man, Paul could certainly move quickly.

Lenore found a relatively rock-free area near the cold, blackened fire ring, and helped Paul spread several layers of blankets there when he came back.

Paul dropped two pillows at one end. "There. Perfect," he announced and eyed Lenore expectantly.

Was he waiting for her approval? "Yes, perfect," she said, and plopped herself down. Now that they were safely back at the campsite, the terror of the canyon drive was receding, and Lenore found she could almost forgive him for dragging her through it. In retrospect, it had been rather extraordinary. Lenore tucked her pillow just the right way under her head and gazed straight up into the heavens.

"Unbelievable," she said. "You know, the people who live out here might be onto something. Look at the difference in the night sky without all those city lights blocking out the stars. I feel like I could almost talk to the man in the moon." And there was definitely something special in the air that night. Lenore felt— She felt Paul lowering himself to her side. She felt his body's heat branding her. Lenore felt—

"Lenore?"

"Yes?"

"It was quite a day, wasn't it?"

"I wasn't all that sure we were going to make it back in one piece," Lenore admitted. She must still have way too much adrenaline wreaking havoc in her bloodstream. At least, she assumed that's why her pulse was racing. She tried several deep, steadying breaths, inhaling through her nose and exhaling out her mouth. Didn't do much that she could notice.

"But here we are, safe and sound."

"Yeah." Lenore guessed so, although she felt decidedly less safe and sound than she had a minute ago.

"Lenore, is it all right if I kiss you?"

He was asking? Lenore tried but couldn't recall any other man who'd bother to do that. It was really rather sweet.

Still, down that road lay nothing but heartache. She knew. "I'd be a fool to say yes," she said, thinking out loud. But while it might not be a wise choice, it was an exciting one. Any calming effect achieved by her deep-breathing exercises had deserted her the instant he'd popped the question.

Paul sighed. "You probably would be. I'm afraid I can't offer much to go along with it. Just the kiss. Commitment is something I'd have to think long and hard about first. I haven't been ready to take on that kind of risk yet. Losing Amanda about killed me."

"I know. A part of me died with my marriage, too. But you know what? I think I'd still like to take a chance on that kiss, Paul."

He levered himself up on one elbow and looked down into her eyes for a long moment, then slowly lowered his mouth to brush hers.

Paul might look like a wild mountain man, Lenore decided. But when it came to the stuff that mattered, the man had finesse. She didn't close her eyes. She couldn't. She needed to see his face while they kissed, to see her hands running through his hair, as well as feel the texture of his beard on her skin and his hair on her hand. It was a moment to be savored.

Paul's beard whisked across her cheeks, and she moaned as his touch kindled a small blaze within her.

Paul tried deepening the kiss, still conscious of try-ing not to overwhelm Lenore. He'd been thinking about this moment ever since he'd met her, but it was still early for her. Lenore was kissing him back, though. His pulse picked up speed as that bit of en-couraging news registered. She was definitely kissing him back.

Was it too soon to bring any of the other male tools of seduction into play now? Last month—two months ago wouldn't have been too soon for him. For so long he'd had nothing but his imagination to go on that the real woman he'd dreamed about actually resting willingly in his arms had his libido jump-started. He ached. His hands itched to discover all her hidden territories. Paul tried to imagine her response to his hand on her stomach. He could start on the prairies and plains of her body and gradually work his way up into the foothills. Yes?

The tight seal holding Lenore's lips together was weakening. He could feel it. If it was too early for his hands, how about his tongue? She sighed and the seal broke altogether. Paul slipped his tongue inside her mouth and found he'd entered paradise. The sanctuary of her mouth was warm and welcoming. He could taste the chocolate mint cookies she'd served for dessert.

Paul was making a meal of her, and Lenore loved every second of it. She'd never felt so beautiful, so wanted. So needed. Delilah, that's who she was. Delilah. Only she had no desire to cut her Samson's hair. Not when he could make her feel like this.

Kissing Lenore had Paul so fired up, he was practically shaking with the effort it took to refrain from a full-scale, step-by-step seduction. Finally, before he did his heart permanent damage, he broke the kiss. He moved lower to gently nip Lenore's neck.

"Your beard," Lenore gasped softly.

"What about it?" Paul asked between love bites.

"It tickles."

"I'll shave it off first thing in the morning," he promised.

"No," Lenore said on a gasp of air as she tipped her head back to make the vulnerable skin of her neck more available. "I like it."

She liked his beard. All right! Maybe she would like his chest, as well. He had a lot of hair there, too. "You do?" he asked and deliberately rubbed her tender skin with his face.

She shivered. "Oh, yes."

He undid the top button of Lenore's shirt and kissed the hollow of her throat. Damn, but this was good and he was hoping for better real soon. He'd wanted to do these things to her and with her for so long. It seemed he'd spent an eternity of nights lying in his solitary bed with his body aching while he'd thought of only this. The real thing came close to being overwhelming. This was how the miners must have felt when they finally struck gold.

Paul moved his fingers to her second button. Lenore shifted beneath his hand. Momentarily, Paul froze. Was she silently objecting? Damn it, no! She couldn't want to stop, not now!

Lenore moved restlessly beneath Paul's touch. He'd probably think she was a brazen hussy if she ripped his T-shirt right off of his body, but it was hard to be coy when your partner wore a pullover-type shirt. Besides, Paul was driving her crazy with his button-by-button seduction. There'd be nothing left but a burned-out shell of a woman by the time he was done with her.

Never having felt this intensely about the subject before, Lenore had no idea how to respond to these wild impulses. Was it even possible to control emotion this strong without bursting something vital?

Paul finally popped the second button, widening the V at the top of her shirt. She blew out a puff of air in relief. Only a few more left to go. Why was he dragging it out like this?

Oh, to heck with it. "Paul?"

"Yeah, honey?"

"Would you take your shirt off?"

He froze briefly then quickly whipped it over his head and off before she could change her mind. The warm June night air felt cool against his heated flesh.

He knew his shoulders were broad and his stomach flat. His line of work took care of that for him. He wasn't worried about being found wanting there. Still, he held his breath until he felt her fingers start to comb through the forest of hair growing on his chest. She liked it. As that last small niggling of self-doubt dissolved beneath her touch, Paul scrambled to release the few remaining buttons keeping him from finding real gold.

This was it.

He thought Lenore's breasts were beautiful. In the pale light cast by the moon and stars, they appeared silver rather than gold, but he knew he'd found real treasure. Paul knelt at Lenore's side, briefly mesmerized by the sight in front of him. Lenore's breasts were fuller than he'd have guessed and tipped with silvery pink pale nipples that peaked from their sudden exposure to the night air as he watched.

He whisked his beard over a nipple and watched in fascination as it peaked even tighter. Then he took her breath away by popping just the tip of its twin into his mouth. He sucked gently, pulling just enough to tease. Could he make her beg for more?

Helplessly, Lenore submitted, unable to move. Yet she felt positively wanton as she reveled in Paul's every touch. A sensual fog slowly enveloped her as she lay there beneath Paul's hot mouth and abrading beard and chest. Paul had train-wrecked her senses. In fact, he was still at it, busily adding insult to injury. She would probably never be able to move again. She'd sue him, provided she ever regained enough strength to contact a lawyer.

One night of pleasure. Would it be such a crime to indulge herself like that? Any minute now, she would find the energy to pleasure Paul in return, Lenore was sure.

She took comfort in the fact that Paul wasn't exactly objecting to her lassitude. Actually, he seemed to be taking a great deal of pride in his workmanship. How like a carpenter. And what hands! She shivered when he leaned back briefly and covered her breasts, warming them with his hands while he took in her half-shuttered eyes and dopey expression. What must he think of her?

Lenore let her eyelids drift the rest of the way closed. They weren't going to live through this vacation anyway. Who cared what he thought of her? She was too far gone to worry. Anything Paul wanted to do to her was okay by her. The man had her burning in a forest fire and she was only too happy to stay there and feel the flames consume her.

Paul kissed her once, briefly.

She would have protested the brevity, only he took her breath away when he immediately went on to thoroughly rub her upper body with his wonderful wiry beard. One of his hands played with the snap at the top of her jeans, and she didn't care. Let it happen. She *wanted* it to happen.

Her breathing deepened when she felt the snap pop. Her eyes still shut, she sucked in oxygen like a prospector rescued from a collapsed mine when she felt Paul easing her zipper down.

"Oh, my God." Lenore jackknifed into a sitting position and clutched at Paul.

"What? What's the matter?" Paul wrapped her in his arms and looked around for some perceived threat. If that damn cowboy who ran this forsaken campground had decided to come calling, Paul would personally pound him into the ground and use him for a tent stake. But first, he had to get Lenore covered. No way was he sharing this particular view with another man.

With one hand, he retrieved her shirt while still blocking any intruder's view of her pinkened breasts with his chest. Hastily, he stuffed her arms into the sleeves and pulled the edges of fabric protectively together. He looked around. Maybe the horses had come back and he'd been too far gone to hear.

But there was nothing to save her from that he could see. "What was it?" he asked as adrenaline made hash of his insides.

Shakily, Lenore wiped her hand over her forehead. "Something ran across my face," she said in a horrified voice. "I think it might have been a mouse or something."

Paul stared at her, eyes wide. His adrenaline was still pumping. He was ready to go to battle for her and he was supposed to duel with a rodent?

Lenore got to her feet, buttoning up her shirt and searching the grass surrounding them as she did so.

"I'm sorry, Paul. I really am. But I can't stay out here any longer. Let's go inside the camper. I think that was just about the grossest thing that's ever happened to me. I mean, whatever it was ran right across my *face.*"

And that, Paul thought as he painfully bent over and picked up the blankets, shook them out and followed, was that. He knew enough about women to know that the mood had been irreparably broken.

The rebirth of his sex life done in by a rodent. See if he ever took Angie to Orlando again.

Chapter Eight

Paul lay on his mattress in the camper counting the small thumps as bugs flew into the exterior light that dimly shone over the camper door. He'd put it on in case anyone rose in the middle of the night and needed to use the facilities. At the time, he hadn't realized how useful it would be.

Three, four, five. It was as good as counting sheep, he supposed, although it didn't seem to be doing much good. His eyes were still wide open.

Six, seven. All good boys will go to heaven. Paul sighed. He'd been within a few minutes of being there anyway. Damn that mouse.

Across from him, Lenore stirred restlessly. Paul was fighting a few tremors of his own, but he doubted they came from a similar cause. Hers were probably rooted in disgust, while his own, well, suffice it to say it wasn't *his* forehead the mouse had run across. He almost wished it had been. He was in *pain* here. But in all fairness to Lenore, Paul supposed some rodent's quick sprint over one's forehead would be as good as a cold shower any day of the week. He just wasn't in the mood to trudge all the way to the shower house at the moment. There might be killer horses or rabid field mice ready and waiting to pounce on an unsuspecting victim.

The night passed. That was about all that could be said for it. It went by. Paul convinced Lenore to put off her box-oven biscuits yet another day. They had a long drive ahead of them and he wanted to get underway.

"You want me to drive for a bit?" Lenore offered when they were two hours down the highway.

"No, why?"

She shrugged. "I just thought you might be getting tired. The glare from the sun can get to your eyes after a while."

"Am I weaving in my lane?" Paul asked, removing his arm from behind her head and his fingers from her hair. He placed both hands on the steering wheel.

"No, you're not," she responded, growing slightly exasperated. "I just thought you might like some relief, that's all."

"Oh." Paul had been worried there for a moment. His eyes weren't tired, and neither was he. Far from it. But he wasn't able to totally concentrate on his driving, either, which was why he'd asked if he'd been weaving.

Lenore had washed her hair before they'd left. The whole car smelled from the apple blossoms of her perfumed shampoo. He felt darn close to being drunk on it and his body was already half-hard. Just what he didn't need after a restless night caused by the same problem. "I'm fine. Just fine." The reassurance was meant just as much for himself as for Lenore.

It took them seven hours to drive from the campground to Great Sand Dunes National Monument. They had to go through one mountain pass, but after Lenore's experience in Phantom Canyon, this was a nonevent, a piece of cake. She barely had to close her eyes at all.

Then, about three in the afternoon, they were there.

"Is this a desert, Mommy?" Timmy inquired as he looked around at the towering piles of sand.

"No," Lenore responded, although it was the best imitation of how she'd always envisioned the Sahara to be that she'd ever seen. "No, as I understand it, the wind scoured some of the rocks in these mountains into sand, and because we're at the juncture of two mountain ranges, the San Juans and the—the—" All she could think of was sangria, but that was a drink. That couldn't be right. "The San Something-or-others—"

"The Sangre de Cristos," Paul supplied smoothly as the four of them stood together in front of the huge mountains of sand while they stretched after the long car ride.

"Thank you," she said, inclining her head civilly in acknowledgment of his help. It was an effort as she still felt awkward around him every time she thought about their lovemaking under the stars. What must he think of her? And there'd been little else to occupy her the past several hours except worrying over her indiscreet and wanton behavior the evening before. Thank goodness for whatever had scampered across her face.

Otherwise, she'd be a heck of a lot worse than simply embarrassed right now.

"You're welcome."

Lenore took a deep breath. "Yes, well, anyway, the sand is trapped here between those two mountain ranges."

"The San Juans and what Mr. McDaniels said."

"Right. And so it sort of swirls around in this corner of the valley and grows higher and higher." Sort of like her desire for Paul.

"Awesome," said Angie. "Wouldn't this be a great place to play King of the Mountain?"

"The best," Timmy agreed, eyeing the seven-hundred-foot drifts.

"Look at everyone wading across that river to get to those dune things. Cool! Let's us go do that." Angie grabbed Timmy's hand and the duo started off.

"Whoa. Hold on, you two." Lenore caught her son by his shoulder and stopped them. "First we have to register at the campground and get things set up. Then we have to ask around and find out what kind of precautions we need to take to safely explore the place."

"Oh, man," Timmy moaned. "That'll take forever."

"Come on, Mrs. Pettit," Angie wheedled. "Look at all those people. Nothing bad's happening to them. Can't we wade across the water now, please? Huh?"

Lenore turned to Paul. Although he'd yet to say anything, she caught him eyeing the oddly pulsing shallow water with a speculative gleam in his eye. "Paul?"

"Hmm? Oh, right. Need to go register. Absolutely. I'm on my way. Be right back. Then we'll go hiking."

Paul took them across the river and up to the base of the dunes after the camper was set up in the park's campground. Lenore supposed she ought to be grateful he didn't take them any farther than that before she'd had a chance to talk to a park ranger. Who knew what horrors lurked in these wilds? Next vacation, Timmy was going to have to settle for something a lot more civilized, Lenore decided then and there. Kiddie Kingdom down by South Bend's Potawatomi Zoo, for example. Everything a child could want was contained in an area about the size of a city block—none of this far-as-the-eye-can-see stuff. A swing set and a swimming pool. What else did anyone need? Really, seven-hundred-foot sand piles were overdoing things a bit in Lenore's opinion. From now on, Timmy was going to have to settle for a sandbox with a foot or two of the stuff in it. After all, what could you do with seven hundred feet of grit that you couldn't do with two? Typical Western overkill.

Fortunately for them, God looks after even the most helpless and least of His creatures and they made it back safely. Later on that night, when Timmy and Angie had been quiet in their beds behind the curtains for quite a while, Paul slipped across the camper from his mattress where he'd been reading, to hers.

"What are you doing?" she whispered in alarm.

He nudged her to give him room. "I just wanted to talk, that's all."

"You can't talk to me from there?" She indicated his own mattress on the other side, but she obligingly scooched over at the same time.

"I didn't want to wake the kids up," he declared nobly as he slid in beside her.

What about her? Didn't he care that she'd just been about to drift off? She was certainly wide-awake now. "What did you want to talk about?"

"This has been a pretty good vacation so far, don't you think?" he asked in what probably passed as a whisper for him.

Lenore put her magazine down. She'd had to turn on her side to accommodate him, so she found herself staring right at him. Lord, he was big. It was curious that she wasn't frightened of him—a man his size could certainly take any sort of advantage of whatever woman he chose. But deep inside of her was the rock-solid knowledge that Paul would never, ever hurt her. He was a man of integrity. An *annoying* man with integrity, but a gentleman in the most meaningful sense of the word. His manners might be a bit rough, but he had a heart of gold. Maybe that was the best way to put it.

Lenore gave in to the sudden urge to kiss him.

"What was that for?"

She shrugged. "Just for being you."

"Ah, well, if that's the case, this one's for being you." And Paul closed the small distance between them and planted a kiss of his own on her soft lips.

"Thank you," she said, already embarrassed by her action. She found it impossible to look into his eyes, so Lenore studied his naked chest instead. Paul slept shirtless; she'd noticed that right away their first night out, and Lenore wondered if the bottoms were a concession for her sake. While they appeared new, they were also loose and comfortable-looking. Why, she could probably slide her hands right under the waistband that barely held that thin cotton to his lean flanks. She shivered in the warm June night.

"But about the vacation...?"

That's right. He'd asked her if she agreed that the vacation was going pretty well. "You think so?" she asked, surprised. Was she the only one convinced they were all going to die? Of course, with the memory of how it felt to be topless with her breasts rubbing up against that incredible chest of his, she could go a happy woman. Embarrassed, but content. "Paul," she said, an unworthy suspicion forming in her mind, "you haven't been putting anything funny into my drinks, have you?"

"What drinks?" he asked carefully as he leaned back to get a better look at her. "We didn't bring anything alcoholic along with us, not even beer. You said it would be a bad example." And no question, he silently added, there'd been times in this frustrating relationship of theirs when he could have used a beer—like now. Why was he torturing himself like this? Why hadn't he had the sense to stay six feet away in his own bed?

Because he'd been in pain over there. Fool that he was, he'd thought it would get better if he could at least hold her a bit, drown his senses in her apple-blossom-scented hair.

Wrong.

Well, maybe a few more kisses might help. He gave in to temptation and kissed her again.

"Stop," she hissed. "The children." Lenore gestured to the curtain next to them.

"They're sound asleep, and I'm in complete control. Don't worry. Even if one of them woke up, all they'd see is a little cuddling."

The kiss hadn't helped, Paul couldn't help but notice when he finished his speech. He was now past pain. It had graduated into a full-fledged agony of wanting.

Lenore, however, was oblivious to Paul's suffering. She was still trying to figure out her own newly discovered and operational libido. It was difficult to believe her body had undergone such a major metamorphosis all on its own. "My milk or orange juice. Did you put anything into either one of those? My mother warned me the night before I left for college to watch out for those fraternity boys. They slipped stuff into unsuspecting girls' drinks that made them crave sex."

"Next thing you knew," Lenore remembered her mother saying, "you'd lost your virginity. And once that happened, well, it was all over. Your husband would be able to tell on your wedding night," she'd said. "He would *know* he wasn't the first, provided, of course, you could interest any man after that." At any rate, the way Lenore had heard it, those fraternity men, interested in only one thing as they were, usually used alcoholic beverages for their nefarious purposes. But Paul wouldn't have had that option here. Like he said, there wasn't even a beer in sight. He would have to make do with her milk or orange juice.

"You're nuts, you know that?"

"No, I'm not. Just cautious. Now did you or didn't you?" Lenore tried to think. It was hard with Paul in such close proximity. The man had a way of making her senses reel. "I can't remember what my mother called it. A Spanish fly? Something Mediterranean." But more to the point. "Paul, did you pledge Greek when you were at Purdue?"

Paul turned on his side and pulled Lenore into his heat. His chin rested on the top of her apple-blossom

hair and he breathed deep while he rubbed her back.
The woman was insane, but it sure felt good to have
her chest up against his like this.

"No, I didn't join a fraternity while I was at Purdue. Satisfied?"

"You could have learned to make this stuff somewhere else, I suppose."

"Would you please stop? It's you. You just like my
kisses. Face it, we're dynamite together." And he
kissed her *another* time just to prove his point.

But, man, what a worrywart.

Paul was doing his best to blunt the effects of that
trait on this trip. Not only did he not want Lenore's
excessive fears to cause the children to miss out on experiencing everything possible during this vacation,
but he didn't want Angie growing up shy and reticent
and afraid of trying new things. He wondered if Lenore appreciated just how hard he was trying. Somehow, though, he guessed now was not the time to ask,
so he lay there and just cuddled her close.

He hung on to his self-control with all his might.
The children *were* too close at hand. But his mind was
fogged from Lenore's nearness.

She was melting. Paul's chest hair tickled her nose
and his hands on her back were divine as they kneaded
muscles stiff from a solid day spent in a car. She decided to forget about the Mediterranean fruit fly, or
whatever it was called. "Never mind," she mumbled,
snuggling closer. "Paul?"

"Hmm?"

"You know, you're a real saint to put up with all
this."

He was just smart enough not to agree with that out
loud.

"You know," Lenore said sleepily, "one of these nights we have to sit down and have a long talk."

Paul tucked her head under his chin and held her close. "Yeah, I know. But not tonight."

"No, not tonight." Her eyes drifted shut. "Good night, Paul."

"Good night, sweetheart."

And then Paul lay there, aching, holding her while she fell asleep on his chest, knowing that she was right. Sooner or later, they would have to talk.

Lenore was an enigma to him. A paradox. A woman strong enough to walk away from a secure but dead-end marriage and raise a son on her own, plucky enough to find her own way when the path of least resistance would have been to remain with her husband, who he gathered had not been abusive, just immature. She could handle the big stuff just fine, yet she fretted over every little petty detail that came her way.

About the only thing Paul really did understand about Lenore and this nutty relationship of theirs was that she sure felt right wrapped in his arms, her hair tangled in with his beard.

Paul was cramped. The upper beds behind the privacy curtains where the two children slept were wider. The adults would have had more room up there, but Lenore had decided she and Paul should sleep next to the doorway, sort of monitor the nighttime traffic. He guessed it made sense; he wouldn't want the kids deciding to find the bathroom by themselves in the middle of the night. But it sure made this kind of thing uncomfortable. Still, there was no way he was returning to his own bunk just yet. Paul had had it with tossing and turning all night, wondering how it would

feel to sleep with Lenore in his arms. Tonight he would
find out. He would just make sure he woke up before
the kids and was properly back in his own place—
alone—before he had a lot of uncomfortable questions to answer in the morning.

"Pssst. Hey, Mr. McDaniels!"

Paul's eyelids shot open. Light shone around the
edges of the canvas flaps they used to cover the plastic windows at night. He heard people shuffling
around outside their camper, smelled bacon cooking
and wood fires burning. Morning had cometh.

"Mr. McDaniels, up here!"

Paul's eyes shifted up and to his left. There he discovered Timmy, eyes wide, head stuck through the
break in the privacy curtain taking in Paul's presence
in his mother's bed with great interest. Damn, he'd
missed making his escape. Now there would be hell to
pay.

"You have a nightmare or something?" Timmy
asked in a whisper.

A nightmare? Sleeping with Lenore certainly hadn't
qualified as that. As a matter of fact, it had been the
first decent night's slumber he'd had in quite a while.
"No, why?"

"The only time Mom lets me get into bed with her
is if I've had a bad dream."

There went his easy out, Paul thought in disgust.
What was wrong with him? He used to be a lot quicker
thinking on his feet than this. The problem, of course,
was that he wasn't on his feet. He was flat on his back.
In bed. With Lenore. She befuddled his brain, that
was it. "Uh..."

"Does Mom know you're still there? She usually makes me go back to my own bed as soon as I'm done being scared."

"Uh..."

All the whispering back and forth awakened Lenore. Slowly and with a great deal of difficulty, her lids fluttered up. "Paul." She breathily greeted the man right under her nose. No wonder she'd been so warm and comfortable last night. Sleeping with Paul was like sleeping with a giant-size heating pad and his chest made a great pillow. She slid her hand up his chest, loving the feel of the pelt of hair on his chest beneath her fingers.

"Good morning, Mom," Timmy chirped cheerfully.

Lenore's eyes widened abruptly and her head swiveled to look behind her. "Timmy! Uh..."

"I got that far," Paul dryly informed her as he captured her wandering hand beneath his own. "I just can't figure out what comes next."

Frantically, Lenore searched her mind for some kind of explanation. It was rough going as sometime during the night, Paul's leg had insinuated itself between her own and was snugly up against the junction of her thighs. Fortunately, one of them—she didn't remember doing it, so it must have been Paul—had awakened long enough to pull a lightweight blanket up over them. At least that little tidbit of parental indiscretion was hidden from Timmy's inquiring gaze. Lenore, however, was exquisitely aware of the situation, and she was having a lot of trouble concentrating on the explanation when the circumstances under the covers were commanding so much attention. "Uh..."

"Your *mother* was having the nightmare, Tim,"
Paul interrupted Lenore's stuttering to smoothly inform the boy after a flare of inspiration for which he
was profoundly grateful. "Not me. That's what happened."

"*I* was having a nightmare?" Lenore asked in
amazement. "Me? I don't—"

"Yes indeed, you had a nightmare. You just don't
remember now that morning's here. It happens that
way sometimes, you know," Paul said knowledge-
ably. He was on a roll now. "That's why I was in bed
with you."

"It was?"

"Yes."

And here she'd taken comfort in the fact that Paul
was obviously falling victim to whatever affliction had
latched on to her and caused her hormones to go on a
rampage. She'd had a nightmare? She didn't know too
many people who'd forgotten something the magni-
tude of a nightmare that had required another body
climbing into bed with them. Of course, how would
she know, sleeping alone the last few years as she had?
In fact, now that she thought about it, she distinctly
remembered Paul's arrival in her bed and she hadn't
been in the midst of any bad dream, either. "Paul—"

"You had a scary dream," Paul informed her
forcefully, ruthlessly cutting her off. He was not going to have this easy way out messed up by any mis-
placed guilty conscience. "That's why we were in bed
together. I was comforting you."

As her sleepiness cleared, the light dawned. "Oh!
Oh, Paul's right. I remember now. I had a bad
dream."

A foot above her, young Timmy propped his chin up with a hand. "Yeah? What was it about?"

"Uh . . ." Back to that again.

"She dreamed we all got a bad case of sunburn when we were out exploring the sand dunes because we didn't take our hats with us. Then we had to crawl home because we forgot to take water and got so thirsty we couldn't even walk anymore."

"I did?"

"That's what you told me."

She tugged on his chest hair and smiled just for him when he flinched. Paul deserved it for all the whoppers he was telling. "Well, you have to admit, it sounds pretty frightening."

"That's why we'll use sunscreen, wear hats, and carry some juice boxes with us this morning," Paul concluded. "You know where the backpack is, Tim? We can put the drinks in there."

Lenore stood in awe of the way Paul smoothly diverted Timmy's attention away from the two of them to the upcoming day's adventures.

Timmy scrambled out of his bed in what Lenore guessed would constitute the eaves of the camper and right over the two of them.

"Oomph!"

"I think the backpack is in the trunk of the car, Mr. McDaniels," he said as he sank a knee into Lenore's back. "I'll wake up Angie, and we'll get dressed while you find it. Maybe we should make a few sandwiches, too, just in case we get lost out there. Starving's probably just as bad as getting thirsty, don't you think?"

"Ow," Paul said as he took an elbow in the face while considering the boy's hypothesis. "I think it takes longer to starve to death than it does to dehydrate, but what the heck, sure we'll throw in a few sandwiches. Why not? We might even save your mom a few nightmares tonight if we do.''

"Wumph," said Paul as Timmy's bony body cleared the bed only to be followed by Lenore's. "Wait a minute, and I'll get out of the way." He made the offer on a gasp of breath as a portion of Lenore's anatomy he would dearly love to become more closely acquainted with in a different time and circumstance rolled over his face.

But Lenore was in no mood to be polite or conciliatory. How like a man to give the woman the nightmares! She gave Paul one last poke in the ribs for good measure as she cleared his body and stood on the floor next to the mattress. "How could you?" she asked in a stage whisper as Timmy pulled back the curtains on Angie's sleeping area. "How can you just make up stories like that about me?"

"Ouch," Paul muttered as he rubbed his sore side. "Are you sure you and Tim only have two elbows apiece? I'd swear I felt a lot more than that." He cranked himself up into a sitting position.

Lenore put her hands on her hips and glared at him. "You deserved every single jab you got. Now kindly remove yourself from my bed. I need to get it folded away and put the table up to eating height if we're actually going to investigate those dunes this morning."

Paul rose, stretched, then rubbed his chest as he shuffled over to his own mattress across the camper floor. "Far be it from me to get in the way of progress," he muttered. "No point. I'd only get steamrollered anyway," he groused as he rooted through his duffel bag for a clean shirt.

It was with equal parts regret and relief that Lenore watched Paul's head clear the shirt opening. That man had a body that could knock every thought she'd ever had right out of her head. She should be grateful he'd covered it up.

Her fingers, however, itched to pull that white knit pullover off again.

Resolutely, Lenore turned her mind to organizing the day. She oversaw breakfast—Paul still didn't want to take time for the refrigerator cinnamon rolls and the box oven—supervised Timmy's and Angie's dressing and teeth-brushing operation and made sandwiches.

She packed the backpack with sunscreen, a first-aid kit, the sandwiches and drinks. She made sure she and the children wore brimmed caps. Lenore left Paul to fend for himself. If he wasn't smart enough to put on a hat, let him get sunstroke. It would serve him right.

Lenore handed the filled backpack to Paul. A big strong man like him certainly ought to be able to lug a little thing like that around without any problems, she told herself as she heartlessly squelched any feelings of guilt.

"Look. Animal tracks just like the ranger said," Angie crowed as she pointed to the sand.

Lenore quickly lowered her gaze to the ground and searched. It was all right. Whatever had made those tracks had had itsy-bitsy feet and she didn't feel too terribly threatened.

"It's hot out here," Timmy complained.

"It's hard walking up and down these hills," Angie said. "My legs hurt and I've got sand in my shoes."

"No point in emptying them until we get back," Lenore informed the child cheerfully as she realized there was little chance they'd wander far enough away

from the nature center to really get lost. It *was* hard
traversing the high, shifting hills of sand. The kids
would not last much longer. "And remember, however far out we walk, we've got to make it that far
back, so save some energy up for the return hike."

"Oh, I'll never make it."

"Can we have the juice boxes now?"

"Gee, who'd want to live in a desert? There's nothing here but sand."

Paul glanced around. The wind ruffled his hair and
beard as he looked into the distance. He could just see
himself as a bedouin sheikh riding across these dunes
on a white Arabian steed. Lenore would be standing
in the middle of the desert, lost, naturally. He would
bear down on her and never slow the horse from a
gallop as he scooped her up and rode off with her into
the setting desert sun. He would avail himself of her
body whenever he felt like it and teach her to speak
only when spoken to. Man, what a hell of an image.

"Daddy?"

"Yeah, pumpkin?"

"Let's go back and wade in the river in front of the
dunes, okay? My feet hurt and my head is sweating
under this hat."

Back to reality, Paul thought with a sigh. He was no
desert sheikh free to steel Lenore away. They both had
responsibilities in the form of one seven- and one
eight-year-old.

Besides, he doubted Lenore would ever be able to
still that tart little tongue of hers. His daydream of a
silent, servile Lenore melted like the mirage it was as
they turned at the top of a dune and followed their
own footprints down to the river and the nature center. By two o'clock, they were back in the car and on

their way west to Mesa Verde and the Four Corners. Paul wasn't too depressed, though. He could think of other ways to still Lenore's tongue, some of them fairly inventive, too.

Chapter Nine

The day hadn't gone at all badly, Lenore decided as the car headed away from Great Sand Dunes National Monument. And even though it was only half over, it was hard to imagine it nose-diving at this point. They were going to spend the rest of the afternoon driving to Mesa Verde to see the ruins of the cliff dwellers. What could go wrong? Out of nowhere, Lenore thought of Phantom Canyon.

"How many mountain passes do we have to go through today?" she asked.

"Same as yesterday," Paul responded. "Just one."

Lenore relaxed again. Just one. She could handle that.

"Of course," Paul continued, "according to the map I was looking at last night, this one's a little bit higher than yesterday's."

"Define 'a little bit,'" Lenore demanded, immediately suspicious.

"Oh, a few thousand feet or so higher."

Or so? She would have asked him to define that, as well, only she really wasn't sure she wanted to know. What it boiled down to was that they were going at least a mile straight up once again without the benefit of wings.

"Just don't think about it," Paul advised.

Easy for him to say. The man didn't appear to have a nerve in his body.

It wasn't that long before the road started doing another snake imitation. They were obviously climbing. Paul switched gears and Lenore knew this was it. Things weren't too bad, although she did have to correct him a few times.

"Look at that view," he would say. "Isn't that the most fantastic thing you've ever seen?"

"Never mind the view," Lenore would respond. "You're supposed to be driving the car."

Paul would grump and humph a bit, but she noticed he kept both hands on the wheel. It made her feel safer, but oddly bereft. She missed his fingers playing in the hair at the nape of her neck.

Then they reached the top of the pass and it was all downhill from there, in more ways than one.

"What's that burning smell?"

"The brakes."

"The brakes?"

"Yeah. Even though I'm in low gear, I'm still having to ride them."

"Are they going to catch fire?"

Paul considered that, but only briefly. "I don't think so. Everything I've heard about mountain driving says this is fairly typical."

It was normal for the brakes to burn? That didn't sound right to Lenore. "Are you sure?" she asked.

"Pretty sure."

Paul sounded slightly on edge himself. That fact spoke for itself and added to her nervousness. She couldn't stop herself from morbidly asking, "What happens if they give out?"

"Well, then we hang on and steer like crazy until we get to one of those runaway things."

This just kept on getting worse and worse. "What runaway things?"

"Haven't you noticed that every now and then there's a cutoff from the main road that doesn't seem to go anywhere? It just ends after a few hundred feet?"

"Like that right there?" She pointed to one of the odd dead ends as it flashed by.

"Yeah. They're paved with sand from what I can tell. I imagine they're mostly for trucks that are running out of control. Driving through all that deep sand slows them down enough so they can stop and wait for the brakes to cool off, I guess."

"Wonderful." Angie and Timmy were in the back seat reliving their morning's adventures and laughing over a grown-up, namely herself, having a nightmare so bad she'd had to have someone crawl into bed with her for comfort.

Lenore cleared her throat. At least they were occupied and she could continue her line of questioning. "I don't suppose you noticed that whoever used that last runaway thing almost didn't stop in time to prevent their smashing head-on into the side of the mountain. The tire tracks go right up to within ten feet of the end of the runaway."

"My guess is that they were made by a truck," Paul said, which indicated he'd noticed, but wasn't about to admit it. "This car is much lighter weight. I'm sure we'd be able to stop in plenty of time."

She was probably wrong, but it almost sounded to Lenore like Paul was reassuring himself along with her. It made her no less nervous, but at least there was a certain sense of kinship at this point that she hadn't felt before.

And quite frankly, there was nothing worse or more destructive than wanting a man—which she did, Lenore had to admit—that she had so little in common with. Okay, so maybe they shared being single parents, but that was about it. Actually, there was one other thing they shared right then. So, she asked herself rhetorically, was it okay to want Paul now that they had being scared in common? Somehow Lenore doubted it. After all, they wouldn't always be spending their time hanging off the edge of a cliff. Northern Indiana was relatively flat after all. She'd have to find some other common ground, and frankly, it wasn't looking hopeful.

"I think we're through the worst of it," Paul said shortly thereafter. "I'm not having to ride the brakes so hard now."

There was a certain amount of fatalism in Lenore's relief, although she was careful not to say anything. But sooner or later, she knew, their luck was going to run out.

Mesa Verde National Park loomed up before them late in the afternoon and Lenore very much feared it was going to be sooner rather than later. "What's this?" she asked as she looked in horror out the windshield. "Who could live in this kind of terrain?"

"Shades of Phantom Canyon," Paul murmured as they fought their way along a narrow road that twisted and backtracked its way up a canyon wall. "Beautiful, though, isn't it?"

"Would you stop with the beautiful?" Lenore demanded. Every time her nerves began settling down, something like this popped up. She hadn't looked closely in a mirror for quite a while, but she wouldn't be at all surprised to find herself considerably grayer when she returned home. "What kind of people built their homes *here?*"

"Come on, Lenore, you did know we were going to see the ruins of cliff dwellings."

"Yes, but I was thinking cliffs maybe twenty-five or thirty feet up. Enough to keep their feet dry when it rained. But these, these are *cliff* cliffs. We're talking thousands of feet here. Are you sure this is the main entrance?"

Paul snorted in irritation. "You want I should try a three-point turn and go back and check the sign at the entrance?"

He had her there. "No. It just seems like a stupid park entrance, that's all," she concluded lamely.

"And by Indiana standards, it is. But this isn't Indiana. I'm getting the definite feeling that people out here have a liking for living life, quite literally, on the edge."

"Very funny."

"Are we almost there yet, Daddy?"

"Yeah, Mr. McDaniels, are we almost there? I'm tired of playing girl stuff."

"Oh, yeah?" sputtered back an indignant Angie. "Well, boy stuff is nasty, isn't it, Mrs. Pettit?"

"Not as nasty as stinky old girl games. Look at this coloring book. *Samantha and her fashion friends.* Whoop-di-do."

"All right, Timothy, that's enough," said Lenore sternly. "If Samantha and her fashion friends aren't exciting enough for you, why aren't you using the book about the dune animals I bought you at the Sand Dunes visitor center?"

"I'm saving it to show at school next fall. I don't want it all colored up."

"Well, that's a choice you're making then, isn't it? You'll just have to deal with Samantha and her fashion friends and be grateful Angie is letting you color in one of her books at all. Something tells me you wouldn't be quite so generous if one of your Power Rangers coloring books was the topic of discussion here."

It never failed. Those two in the back seat had some kind of built-in radar. They got along fine during a ride until some innate inner sense told them they were only fifteen or twenty minutes away from their destination. It was too close for Paul to bother stopping the car and disciplining them and therefore safe for them to let things degenerate into name calling. At least, Lenore guessed that was what was going through their mischievous little minds. Who could really tell with kids?

"The campground is right up this road a few more miles, folks. Just hang on. We'll all be able to get out and stretch in another fifteen minutes."

If the campground was on terrain anything like this entrance, Lenore would just have to make sure they didn't stretch too far when they began working out the kinks from this long car trip. She wouldn't want anyone tumbling off the edge of one of these precipices during an overly exuberant side twist.

But when they were finally settled in, Lenore was relieved to find the campground was relatively flat.

"This isn't so bad," Lenore said as she looked around.

"No," Paul agreed. "My guess is that we're on a fairly broad mesa top."

"Can we go find the cliffs now, Mr. McDaniels?" Timmy asked. "Can we?"

Lenore's heart sank. Leave it to the males in the crowd to agitate. They couldn't stand being safe or sitting still for even ten minutes. The sun was setting and she wanted nothing more than a warm shower and what passed for a bed in their borrowed camper.

She was also, however, getting smarter. "Great idea," Lenore said instead of trying to put the kibosh on the suggestion. "Let's go do it. Nothing like seeing the sun set over the Anasazi ruins. Very romantic, I imagine. We'll all hold hands while we walk through them, or you can hang on to my shirttails so you don't trip on anything in the dark. It's a long way down, you know. And, hey, we can eat dinner around nine or ten tonight, no problem. You guys probably aren't very hungry anyway, are you?"

Paul looked at her as though she'd momentarily taken leave of her senses, obviously missing her reverse-psychology ploy entirely. "Lenore, the main ruins are another who knows how many miles down that road you were objecting to just a short while ago. I don't want to drive on it after dark unless we have to. The park rangers are presenting a nature talk tonight here at the campground. I thought we'd eat some dinner, go to that, and hit the hay."

See? Were men predictable, or what? They always wanted to do the exact opposite of whatever you said. It would be funny if it wasn't so sad that she found herself once again falling like a rock for one of the contrary species. "Oh, but, Paul—"

He interrupted firmly, "We'll go to the ruins in the morning, when it's light and we can actually see something." Then he offered his olive branch. The old carrot-on-a-stick routine. "Maybe tomorrow we can have the refrigerator biscuits cooked in the box oven for breakfast."

Lenore almost snorted. Did she look stupid? She should live so long. He would have some sort of excuse ready by morning, she was sure. Lenore decided not to tell him that she'd thrown the tube of sweet biscuits out that morning. It had gone so long past the expiration date, it had burst open on its own, virtually begging to be cooked. But there'd been no time to make them, of course, so she'd had to toss them. Wait till she threw that in his face come morning.

Lenore sighed in mock disappointment instead. Let him think he'd ruined her day. A little guilt was good for a man. "Well, if that's the way you want it, I suppose I'd better get dinner going."

"We'll all help," he declared, looking at her as though he wanted to take her temperature.

Well, why not play along? "Actually," she prevaricated, "all I had planned was hamburger goulash cooked in that cast-iron bucket over the open fire. I bet you three could whip that up without any problem while I go for a short walk." She put her fingers to her temples. "I feel a bit of a headache coming on. A walk might clear it up."

"Oh, well, sure. We can do that. I guess."

Lenore gave Paul a brilliant smile. "Good. The hamburger meat's in the cooler. I'll be back in a little while. Bye." And she turned and walked away.

She ambled through the campground, relishing the solitude for the first ten minutes, then feeling lonely and even a bit immature after that. She headed back to their own site.

She'd been gone maybe twenty-five minutes total. Richard would have been a blubbering idiot by then had she ever pulled a similar stunt on him. But Paul— Paul had the fire going and Lenore could smell the meat simmering in the pot he had suspended over it. The children had the nearby picnic table spread with a cloth and Timmy was busily setting places at it while Angie filled a plate with cut-up carrots and broccoli florets surrounding a small cup of dip.

Paul got under her skin at times, she thought to herself, but he was not Richard. He had everything beautifully organized and under control.

"I'm impressed," she said.

"Good," Paul grunted, examining her face. "You feeling any better?"

Not really. She felt stupid now, for leaving him to do all this. "Yes," she said.

"Go lie down anyway," he directed gruffly. "No point taking a chance on having that headache come back. We'll call you when dinner's ready in a few minutes."

"I'd rather help out here." Now it was her turn to be perverse. Lenore didn't want to be banished to her bed, even if it was out of Paul's thoughtfulness for her. She wanted to be with them.

"No, go ahead and lie down. There's nothing for you to do here anyway. We've got it all under control." And in a display of gentlemanly behavior, Paul pulled open the camper door and held it for her.

What could she do? She went in and lay on the mattress. Arms folded over her chest, Lenore grumpily stared up at the vent in the ceiling. It was true, Paul did have everything under control. She was decidedly superfluous right then, unnecessary baggage.

So what?

What did she have—some kind of need to be needed? Was she a martyr?

Probably. After all, Lenore had never seen herself as the decorative type, and certainly in her marriage with Richard, had never had the opportunity to pursue the role. Being in charge, making all the decisions, never being able to take a break from all the responsibility had grated—a lot—but it was also the only role she'd known.

She found it equally grating never to have the final word on this vacation of theirs. More apropos, she guessed, would be to say she'd been demoted to an Indian after a long run at being chief. It was surprising how equally odious Lenore was finding that new position. There was also the unpleasant possibility that Lenore was turning out to be one of those disagreeable sorts, the perennial malcontent.

How was that for a depressing moment of self discovery?

"Lenore?" Her name came on a whisper as Paul quietly opened the camper door and stuck his head inside.

She sat up immediately, grateful for the reprieve from her thoughts. "Yes?"

"I didn't want to wake you if you'd fallen asleep, but dinner's ready."

Lenore hopped out of bed. "I'll be right there."

"Okay." Paul withdrew his head and Lenore scuttled out the door behind him, anxious to rejoin her untraditional family. Even an hour had been too long when spent entirely in her own company, which didn't say much for the kind of companion she must make.

The goulash was good—for goulash. Lenore was lavish with her compliments. The cleanup was accomplished without her, Paul and the two children still solicitous to the extreme in their concern over her nonexistent headache. Lenore didn't like being pigeonholed as the do-nothing guest any more than she'd cared for the maid role, but she was afraid to complain for fear of being banished to her bed once again. There had to be a happy medium somewhere, didn't there?

And couldn't she ever have a say in what role she played?

Why did her lot in life always seem to be crammed down her throat, whether she liked it or not?

Lenore helped Paul dry and stow away the last of the utensils while she thought about that.

"You all ready to go hear the ranger's talk?" Paul asked when they'd finished.

"Is it going to be long and boring?" Angie asked suspiciously.

Lenore tried to see it from a child's perspective. "I don't know," she finally admitted. She was more concerned with keeping track of where Paul was storing the dinner supplies. There was a real possibility she would never be able to find anything again by the time he was done—providing, of course, she was allowed back in her kitchen.

"How could it be boring?" Timmy asked as they set off for the designated talk spot. "There's so much neat stuff here to get explained about, even if it's long, it won't be boring."

"Right." Paul nodded his head. "I agree."

Timmy grinned up at him and reached for Paul's hand. Paul clasped it in his without hesitation. Angie dropped back a step and took Lenore's.

"Men," Angie said with a womanly sniff. "What do they know?"

Lenore thought her extremely perceptive and she swung their coupled hands between them for the remainder of the short walk.

Once at the outdoor theater, they settled down on the available primitive seating and prepared to listen.

The talk began and the ranger discussed the park's plant and animal life rather than the Anasazi themselves. The cliff dwellers would be covered during the tours of their ancient ruins, he explained before jumping into an enthusiastic discourse on the park's copious number of tarantula spiders.

"Do you think that's true?" Lenore leaned against Paul a while later and whispered the question.

Paul shrugged and she felt the ripple transfer to her own body. She was still dealing with that when he whispered back, "Why would he lie?"

"Yes, but it's such an awful picture. Tarantulas that go for group runs around the park."

"He says it's beautiful—an awesome sight to see."

"Beauty's in the eye of the beholder, Mom," Timmy joined in piously. "You said so yourself."

Lenore guessed she had, she thought rather unhappily. But nobody was going to convince her that tarantulas running en masse, enough of them to black out the roadways, was an awe-inspiring sight. Terrifying, yes. But awe inspiring? Not in her book. "Do you really think there are that many of them around here to literally cover the ground in all directions the way he said?"

Once more Paul shrugged and again Lenore felt an answering shiver travel right down to her toes. Damn the man.

"Daddy," Angie begged, "can I sleep in your bed with you?"

No, she couldn't, Lenore wanted to say. Because she would be sleeping there herself tonight. No way was she going to sleep alone. At least, if she shared a bed with Paul, the tarantulas would be provided with a bigger target. Surely they would choose him to bite, wouldn't they?

"No, sugar," Paul answered quietly. "You're too big to sleep in bed with me now, remember?"

"But what if the tarantulas pick my bed to run over?"

"What if they pick mine, and you're in it?"

"Don't worry, Angie," Timmy said, evidently having forgiven the little girl for inflicting Samantha and her fashion friends on him. "We'll close everything up tight and I'll check all over the camper before we go to bed tonight and plug up any holes. That way, if the spiders pick tonight to go for a run, and we're in the way, they'll have to go up and over the roof—or I guess they could go underneath, couldn't they? But they won't get us."

"Oh. Good idea. Thanks, Timmy."

"You're welcome."

Lenore kept a nervous eye on the sides of the road as they walked back to the camper when the talk ended, but couldn't make out much of anything but rough outlines in the deep country dark. She was very, very careful where she set each foot down and she sincerely hoped she didn't have to go to the bathroom in the middle of the night. No way was she leaving the camper before morning.

But morning's light, instead of dispelling her worries only served to deepen them.

"You have to be kidding."

"Don't be such a wuss."

"I am not a wuss. I happen to be the only one here displaying any common sense. This place is unbelievable. No wonder they all left." Lenore stood at the entrance to one of the cliff-dweller ruins, her arms stubbornly crossed in front of her, and refused to take one more step.

Paul eyed the balking woman beside him and considered his various options. He decided to try reassurance first. "This is the most tourist-friendly Anasazi site there is. If you don't see these things here, you'll never get up the nerve to see them anyplace else."

Lenore was unmoved. "I will probably also never try bungee jumping off the Empire State Building. Somehow I don't see it as much of a loss."

So much for reassurance.

"Mom, you're holding everybody up behind us."

"Well, pardon me all to pieces. I'd step to the side, only it's about a ten-million-foot drop-off over there, and I don't trust that one lousy little metal pipe they put up as a guardrail to save me."

"You've got to at least let us by, Mom."

Lenore looked at her son, her eyes narrowed. "What makes you think I'm letting you go, either?

This place isn't safe. Anybody can see that." She glared at Paul. "Did you bother to ask how many tourists they lose per day before dragging these poor innocent children out here?"

Paul was fast losing his patience. "Listen, lady, you seem to have forgotten that this whole trip was your idea. I've about had it with your cold feet every time we go to do something. I can't believe you'd drive all this distance to get here and then not be willing to try to overcome your fears long enough to see these things."

Lenore took a cautious baby step backward and turned sideways. Immediately, people began streaming past. What was wrong with all of them? Couldn't they recognize danger when it was right in front of their eyes? She put a hand on Paul's chest in a pleading gesture. Immediately, she felt his heart beating beneath her palm, and warmth seeped up the length of her arm. Darn the man! And darn her own traitorous body that she could react like this with such a stubborn, myopic son of a gun.

She tried to explain herself one more time. "Listen, I think I already told you how I felt. When they said cliff dwellers, I assumed maybe twenty-five, thirty feet up. But this—" Lenore gestured helplessly to the scene in front of them "—this is just crazy."

Paul gazed stonily down the trail, then back at her, unmoved. "If it was all that dangerous, if people died here on a regular basis, they'd have closed the place down." Couldn't she see that? Meanwhile, the kids were getting impatient, they were losing valuable time, and she was making a fool out of herself in front of the children. It was up to him to see that Lenore didn't do anything here that she would regret later on.

Lenore wasn't getting through to him. She made one more desperate attempt. "Paul, all the inhabitants disappeared from here. Doesn't that tell you something? They say it's a mystery, but the answer is right in front of our eyes. Just look!" She waved at the path in front of them. "Do you see where this is taking us? To an itty-bitty ledge halfway up an extremely high precipice. I ask you, where's the mystery? It's my guess that one by one they woke up thirsty in the middle of the night and got up for a drink of water. They were sleepy, disoriented, took one little misstep, and boom, they're over the edge and goners. Can't you see it? And now we're all following along in their footsteps!"

The woman was on the verge of becoming hysterical, Paul decided. There was no reasoning with her. He grabbed her arm and began to tow her behind him. "You're coming."

Lenore dragged her heels, but she was no match for Paul's strength. "I'm not, and neither are they."

"Of course they are. Who knows what kind of trouble they'd get up to if we let them out of our sight while we saw the ruins? Come on, kids," he directed.

"Mr. McDaniels?" Timmy began, a worried question sounding in his voice.

"Are you sure we should make Timmy's mom come, Daddy?" Angie asked as they trailed behind him.

"Don't worry," Paul reassured them. "She'll thank us for this later."

"I won't," Lenore said, frowning in disappointment as she failed in her attempt to kick him in the shins. "In fact, I have every intention of exacting a terrible retribution."

"I can hardly wait," Paul informed her. "Now stop making a scene. You're scaring the children."

She was the one scaring the children? Lenore would kill him for that. Resistance being futile, she allowed Paul to drag her along and hung on to him for dear life. If she fell over the edge, she was darn well going to take him down with her.

The rest of their visit proceeded along similar lines. She was more or less forced into visiting other sites in the park even less user friendly than the first. They involved climbs up and down cliff faces using the original Anasazi footholds and handholds with only the addition of a chain thrown down the cliffside for additional safety. She was determined to live through it all strictly to have the pleasure of murdering Paul herself when they got back to South Bend. And to think she'd actually been sexually attracted to the man!

Miraculously, they left Four Corners and Mesa Verde in one piece, then proceeded to torture themselves and the car through other mountain passes as they headed upstate. Dinosaur National Monument was a blur. Lenore didn't believe for a minute that this absurd, jagged vertical landscape they'd been passing through had ever been grassy lowlands where dinosaurs roamed, but she was concentrating too heavily on survival by that time to comment.

"Isn't this place awesome?" Timmy asked as he watched in wide-eyed wonder while paleontologists exposed ancient animal bones right in front of their eyes.

Even Lenore was impressed. "Yes," she said. As far as Lenore was concerned, it was the best of both worlds. Somebody, some paleontologist with brains, had at last had the foresight to design the visitor center to enclose the mountainside. The workers and everybody else got to enjoy a national monument in air-conditioned comfort and without the possibility of a horde of tarantulas going for a midnight run. "This is my kind of place," Lenore announced as she glanced around with pleasure.

Paul rolled his eyes at Angie and Timmy, who laughed. "Finally," they all chorused.

She stuck out her tongue at the lot of them.

Paul chuckled once more and threw a companionable arm around her shoulder as they led the children around to read the signs posted at the various stations.

And then—then their vacation was over. Lenore was relieved and saddened both. For those ten days, they'd really been a family. She would miss that closeness. Both with Paul and Angie. But she and Tim would still see them, Lenore was sure. In fact, maybe she would have Paul and Angie over for a barbecue when she got her pictures back sometime next week. That would be nice.

They drove through more horrendous mountain passes, then the mountains ended as abruptly as they'd started a week ago. For two days after that, they followed the flat, straight asphalt ribbon of Interstate 80. Miraculously, they recrossed the Mississippi River with all four of them still alive and nobody in a body cast.

The constriction that she'd felt tighten around her chest when Timmy had first come up with this crazy plan finally loosened and she was able to draw her first deep breath in over a month. They had persevered.

They had survived. They were within shouting distance of home.

The children were sleeping like little angels in the rear seat of the car. Lenore thought maybe she'd catch forty winks herself.

Chapter Ten

Lenore let her eyes drift closed. Why not? The party would be over soon enough. Surely there was nothing wrong with letting Paul guide them the final leg of their journey. He'd certainly commandeered control the rest of the time they'd been together and, much as she hated to admit it, done a good job of it.

And besides, Lenore thought as she yawned and nestled into the corner formed by the seat and door, she'd have control of her life back soon enough. Just a few more hours, in fact, she assured herself as her mind began to shut down.

"Lenore?"

Paul spoke quietly, but Lenore's name ricocheted around the interior of the quiet car.

Her eyes popped open. "What?"

"I thought that now, while the kids are asleep, might be a good time for you and me to talk."

Talk? "About what?"

Paul shrugged one shoulder, but didn't turn his head. He kept his eyes on the road. "You and me. Us."

Uh-oh. "Us?" she squeaked, then cleared her throat. "Us?" she questioned again in a voice closer to her own. Her slouch had straightened out all by itself. Her posture in the seat was now as rigid as if she'd been laced into a whalebone corset. "What about us?"

"I thought this whole camping trip thing went pretty well, didn't you?"

Okay, she cautiously agreed, she'd give him that. "Yes."

"And before that, we had fun doing things with the kids, too."

If you didn't count some of the silly squabbles that would have blown up between any two kids trying to establish their pecking order. "Well, yes."

"I've never thought much about remarrying," Paul admitted.

"Me, neither," Lenore quickly interjected, lest he be headed where she thought he was headed.

But Paul seemed so intent on getting out what he wanted to say, he was oblivious to her response and just kept on talking. "I mean, one minute you're on top of the world, you've got it all. Then the next, all you've got left is an ache so bad, it about tears your gut right out."

Paul's hands whitened around the steering wheel. "I meant what I said earlier, that I'm glad Amanda didn't suffer. But you were right. I wish I could have said goodbye or something."

And maybe something a little more than just goodbye? Lenore wondered sympathetically.

"The thing is, I was never much good at getting out the words a woman wants to hear, you know what I'm saying? I always figured Amanda knew, though. I mean, I married her, didn't I? At least, I hope to God she knew."

"I'm sure she understood, Paul." But for herself, Lenore knew she'd want the words and she'd never get them from Paul.

Paul put on his blinker and steered around a semi-trailer. "Look at that thing sway," he said. "Now there's something I'd actually like to see a government study on—just how safe are those monsters?" He watched it recede in the rearview mirror. "Anyway," he went on brief moments later, "after Amanda was killed, I figured it would be better—easier just to fly solo from then on. I sure as hell never wanted to go through having the bottom drop out on me again. If you haven't got anything to lose, what's to lose?"

"But now you feel differently?" Lenore asked weakly.

Paul shifted restlessly behind the wheel. He honked at a minivan straddling the lane line. "Remember that night we made Angie's muumuu?"

How could she ever forget? "Yes, I remember."

"It got me thinking, remembering how good it was to have somebody special around who genuinely liked being around my kid—"

"Angie's a delight."

"Yeah, well, so's Tim. The thing is, the two of them really get along."

Mmm, maybe. "For the most part," she allowed.

"And you and I get along."

Uh...

"You've got to admit, we're dynamite in at least one area. If it hadn't been for that damn mouse that night..."

Lenore cleared her throat and hastily checked the back seat. Timmy and Angie were still out cold. "Yes, well, as to that—"

"And you don't have to worry that I'm just trying to replace Amanda. I enjoy being around you—a lot, just like I did her, but it's different, I swear. You're nothing like each other."

That was about as close to a declaration of love and undying devotion as she was likely to get from a man like Paul. Lenore massaged her forehead with her fingers in an effort to jump-start her brain, which was currently lolling around inside her cranium without a thought to call its own. She hadn't been expecting this. It had always been her understanding that men were not big on commitment. She'd thought they'd just stay friends. Friendship was safe—Lenore would have made sure it was safe. But this? She assumed Paul was leading up to a marriage proposal. Now how could she make him understand her own deep aversion to the institution?

"Paul, before you go any further, maybe I should tell you about my first marriage."

"You were young," he interjected quickly. "A lot of early marriages don't make it. I wouldn't be too hard on yourself, if I were you."

"Thank you. I try not to be." Lenore pointed out the windshield. "Watch out for that guy. See how he's all over the road?"

"I'm watching, I'm watching."

"I think he's been drinking."

"I said I'm watching him, so quit worrying. I'm in control."

"That's just the problem," Lenore burst out as Paul edged past the weaving car.

"What? What's the problem? Look, we're safely past him."

"That's not the point."

That surprised him. "It isn't? Then what is?"

Lenore self-righteously crossed her arms over her chest. "It's this whole control thing."

Paul risked a sideways glance at her. "What whole control thing? You wanted to get safely past that car. I got you safely past it. Where's the problem?"

"Would you forget about passing that car? That's not what I'm talking about."

His eyes really widened at that. "If we weren't discussing my ability to pass safely, what were we talking about?"

"Your need to always be in control."

"Of course I need to be in control. I'm the one driving. What did you want me to do? Pull the steering wheel off and hand it over to you?"

Lenore's arms remained virtuously crossed as she glared at him. "You just don't get it, do you?"

"Evidently not," Paul grated from behind clenched teeth. "You want to lay it out for me? Plain English would help."

"Look," Lenore said. "You were right. Richard and I were too young when we got married. We were kids playing house. It was a lot of fun. Then Timmy came along and I had to grow up and be a real mother. Richard never made the transition. Every decision, every responsibility, every task around the house fell to me. I couldn't take it anymore."

"But you just said—"

"I know what I just said. I'm getting to that."

"I'd forgotten about this part of being around a woman," Paul muttered, but it was loud enough for Lenore to hear. "Half the time a man has absolutely no clue what they're talking about. Please continue," he said more loudly. "I'm all ears."

"I'm trying to make a point here—"

"Could have fooled me," he growled.

"As I was saying," Lenore continued determinedly, "I hated having all the responsibility."

"Now just a minute. Just a darn minute. I did my best to take as much of the burden of this trip off you as I possibly could. I was a damn paragon, bending over backward to make things easy for you. Don't you dare equate me with that husband of yours."

"I'm not. Don't you see?"

Paul rolled his eyes. Here they went again. "See what? I see that I've done the exact opposite of everything you objected to from Richard and you're still complaining. That's what I see."

Lenore nodded vehemently. "That's exactly it."

Amazed by her response, Paul thought back over what he'd just said. Something in it had struck a chord within Lenore. Damned if he knew what. He sighed tiredly. "I'm afraid you're going to have to spell it out, Lenore. I still don't get whatever point it is you're trying to make."

"Richard was one extreme, you're the other. With him, I got stuck making all the decisions. With you, I never get to make any."

"All the decisions I made on the trip worked out, didn't they?" Paul asked defensively.

"That's not the point."

"Then what in hell is?"

"Shh, you're going to wake the children."

"Sorry," he said only a bit more quietly. "So what is?"

"I'm not interested in extremes! That's the point. If I ever decide to get involved with somebody again, it's going to have to be with somebody interested in a partnership. Someone willing to make decisions by consensus."

They were on I294 by then, passing the city of Chicago. Two more hours, max, to straighten things out between them. Paul wondered if it would be enough.

"If I hadn't forced you to see those ruins, you never would have done it by yourself. Admit it."

"I admit it."

"Aren't you glad you saw them?"

"In retrospect, yes. But that's not what I'm getting at here."

Paul ground his teeth. "Aargh." What had seemed so clear only a short time ago—that he and Lenore and their two children belonged together—was now suddenly all jumbled up once more. Did he really want to spend the rest of his life with a woman who didn't appreciate how hard he'd tried to make her happy? Was a simple thank-you for all his effort asking too much? Evidently so. "Listen, Lenore, maybe we both need a little space about now. You know, time to think things through, decide what we really want from each other."

She knew what she wanted. A declaration of love and a willingness to share decisions responsibly. She didn't want a husband who ruled by decree.

"I must have misread the situation," he went on. "I thought you had come to, you know, care for me." At least he didn't think it was like her to be so lavish with her affection as they'd been on a few occasions during the trip. Not without some degree of involvement. But what did he know?

"I have," she said simply. "But just like you didn't want to open yourself up to the chance of more hurt, I don't want to chance any more misery. What good is being in love if we end up miserable?"

Is that what she thought? That loving him would end up with her doing some kind of hurt dance? Paul didn't get his feelings hurt too often. Most of the time he wasn't even aware he had any, but he was aware of them right then and they were smarting. "So are you saying you don't want to see me anymore?" That would break Angie's—and his—heart.

That panicked her. Never see him again? When he put it like that— "No!" She squirmed in her seat. "But maybe, like you said, maybe we should take a little break, think about things." She should cut their relationship off here and now. It would probably hurt less in the long run to give him up cold turkey, just as people gave up cigarettes and other addictive things, but she couldn't bear to.

"Fine," he grunted. That old played-out mine back in Cripple Creek, what was it? Oh, yeah, the Bonanza would come back to life and into full production before Paul McDaniels served up his heart on a silver platter for Lenore Pettit to carve up again, that was for darn sure, Paul promised himself.

The rest of the trip down the Indiana toll road was completed in silence.

That silence stretched out a long time—until it was time for Lenore to help Paul with the end-of-the-month books again.

Lenore was looking forward to seeing him again. She'd missed him—badly. Only Paul never showed his face, not once for two straight days. "Coward," she muttered as she stomped off that last afternoon.

Halfway through July, she'd thought of a million reasons to call him and grovel. She was still miserable and wanted him any way she could get him. "Wouldn't it be better to be unhappy with him than without him?" she asked her dresser mirror one night before climbing into her lonely bed. "I mean, heck, you're unhappy anyway, so what the hey?" But she couldn't do it, she just couldn't. "And besides," she told herself, "Paul's not exactly beating down your door, now is he? Obviously, he doesn't miss you the way you miss him. Forget him." And maybe by the time she was sixty, she would.

After an interminable length of time, much longer than she ever remembered July taking up before, the month finally ended. She went back to McDaniels Construction once again to help Barb run the end-of-the-month payroll and fill out the monthly government forms.

"So," she casually asked around two in the afternoon, "where's Paul today?"

"Who knows?" Barb responded. "But wherever it is, he should only stay there. He's been snarling around here like a rabid dog the past few weeks, ever since he got back from that vacation of yours, in fact. Come to think about it, he didn't show his face in the office the end of last month, either. Something happened between you two on your trip, right? And now you can't face each other." Barb snapped her fingers. "That's it, isn't it? Are you pregnant or something?"

"Good grief, no!"

"Well, something went wrong on that trip and I—"

The shrill ring of the telephone interrupted them and Lenore gratefully grabbed for it. "Good afternoon. McDaniels Construction. Mr. McDaniels isn't in right now. He usually calls in for messages every few hours. May I have him return your call? Lenore Pettit? Speaking. What? Oh. Oh, my. Yes. I'll be right there. Thank you for calling." Lenore hung up without saying goodbye.

Barb gave Lenore a puzzled look when she stood and began rooting through drawers. "What's up?"

"Some little boy at Angie's day camp struck out during a softball game. He lost his temper and threw his bat. Angie was in the on-deck circle and got hit in the face with it. Her cheek is split open and her new permanent front teeth are loosened. Evidently Paul put me down as the emergency contact on the health form in case he couldn't be reached. Darn, I can't think right now. Do you remember where I stuck my purse when I came back from lunch? I've got to get to the hospital."

Barb found the purse that Lenore had slung over the closet doorknob and handed it to her. Lenore stared at her, a bit wild-eyed. "Thanks. See if you can find Paul. I suppose it's too much to ask that he'd be wearing his beeper, but try it. Then call his car phone number. Do whatever you have to do, but don't stop until you've located him. I'm leaving for the hospital right now. Have him go right there."

Lenore caught just about every stoplight it was possible to catch on her way across town. Even so, she was beside Angie's hospital cot in under twenty-five minutes. The privacy curtains around Angie's small cubicle in the emergency room were still swaying when Lenore took the little girl's hand in hers.

Before Lenore could ask how she was doing, Angie burst into tears. "I'm so glad you c-c-came," she sobbed. It broke Lenore's heart that she'd had to be alone for even the time it had taken Lenore to cross town. Damn all traffic engineers *and* their stupid traffic-control plans. Damn the lights themselves, too, for that matter.

Gingerly, she brushed Angie's bangs back from her forehead. "I got here as fast as I could," she assured Angie. "And as soon as Barb finds your dad, he'll be here lickety-split, too. Now don't you worry about a thing. I'll find out what it's going to take to fix you up and get you out of here."

"L-Lenore?" Angie gulped her name.

"Yes, sweetie?"

"It hurts."

Lenore nodded in understanding. "I know."

Fresh tears bubbled out of Angie's eyes. "And I wanna go home," the child wailed softly. "I wanna g-go home right now!"

And Lenore would have done anything to comply with Angie's wishes, but she'd had enough experience with Timmy's various cuts and scrapes to know that while the wound on Angie's face certainly wouldn't qualify as life threatening, it would definitely take a few stitches to close it up. Lenore turned to the day-camp director who'd ridden in the ambulance and stayed with Angie up until then. "Has the doctor been in to see her yet?" she asked.

"Yes. He left to see to a few things, but he said he'd be right back."

Lenore nodded. And, in fact, only a few minutes went by before he returned. That was when Lenore knew she was officially old. Everybody knows how long it takes to get through medical school, and this—this kid in the white doctor's coat was quite definitely younger than she was. Why, to use one of her grandmother's old sayings, he was barely dry behind the ears. This child *couldn't* be a doctor. He'd probably have to prop the textbook up in front of him to consult with while he worked on her beautiful little Angie. And that was how Lenore thought of her, she realized at that moment. As hers. Paul, too, for that matter. Darn it, she loved them both. The break with Paul had come too late to save her heart. Lenore wondered if Paul thought of Timmy as his? How about herself?

Well, she would make Paul sit down and they would deal with all that later. Right now, she had a traumatized child and an underage M.D. to deal with.

Lenore's eyes narrowed as they focused on the young man in front of her.

Over her dead body would he touch Angie.

The doctor wanna-be introduced himself.

Lenore nodded curtly in response to the introduction. "Dr. Conrad." Frankly, she wouldn't have been surprised if he'd said he was Doogie Howser. He asked Lenore to step outside the cubicle. She made sure to stand where Angie could still see her, but not really hear her conversation with the good doctor.

Dr. Conrad began to inform Lenore of the arrangements he'd been making. It seemed a maxillofacial surgeon who was some kind of glorified dentist specializing in facial trauma was still in the building after just finishing up with a car-accident victim. Young Dr.

Conrad had made arrangements for her to check on Angie before she left.

"There are a lot of things that can happen here," Dr. Conrad warned. "Of course, we'll x-ray—make sure her jaw isn't broken. But I really don't think it is. Probably you'll just get a recommendation to see a good pediatric dentist, who will explain the various possibilities to you. The teeth may tighten up by themselves and be just fine, or the nerves may have been too severely traumatized and they'll die. Then she might need a root canal on one or both front teeth." Dr. Conrad shrugged. "Another possibility is wiring her teeth in place until they're stable again. I really don't know."

Lenore was not surprised.

"Meanwhile, we'll also get an X ray of her cheek-bone, although again, I'm not expecting any fractures to show up. Still, it's better to be safe than sorry."

It was hard to argue with that.

"Meanwhile," the doctor continued cheerfully, "I've got my equipment right here, and as soon as we've got the go-ahead from the radiologist, I'll suture up this spare hole in the cheek Angie seems to have developed. Before you know it, she'll be almost as good as new."

He smiled an anticipatory kind of smile that included Lenore, but concentrated mostly on Angie lying on the cot in the cubicle. It seemed like he was almost pleased the little girl was hurt so he could practice his stitching techniques on someone too young to know any better. That and his use of the word *almost* really got Lenore's blood boiling. The guy was a bit too eager. If he was given his way, Le-

nore suspected that Angie would walk out of the ER
looking like Frankenstein's monster, with stitches from
ear to ear whether she needed them or not.

Well, Dr. Howser, uh, Conrad, would just have to
wait for another victim to practice on. Paul might not
be here to protect his baby from the mad scientist getting ready to operate, but by God, Lenore was. And as
much as she hated confrontation of any sort, she
would make sure Angie got the best possible care until Paul arrived to take over. She would do this for Paul
and Angie, because she loved them both, and it was a
hell of a time for personal revelations to take place,
but what could she do?

"This maxillofacial whatever—just what are his or
her credentials?"

"Oh, she's very good," the doctor assured her.

"Then she's board certified in her specialization?"
Lenore pressed, not willing to give an inch in her quest
for the best for Angie.

"Um, I'm not exactly sure about that," he admitted, brows knitting together as he tried to think. Evidently, it was an effort.

"Why don't we go out and ask at the desk?" Lenore suggested grimly. "And while we're there, let's
see if they can find us a board-certified plastic surgeon with a specialization in facial plastic surgery and
hopefully some exposure to microsurgical techniques
to put in the sutures."

Dr. Conrad looked panicky at that. He probably
had a lot of victims try to escape his clutches. He
wasn't going to let this one go without a struggle.
"Mrs. McDaniels, I'm perfectly capable of closing
Angie's wound. Your daughter's upset and wants to go
home. It'll take quite a while to get a specialist in here.

If I do the job, you'll be out of here in half, one-third the time."

This was going to be a battle, Lenore just knew it. She didn't even think to correct his assumption that she was Mrs. McDaniels. The title felt right. "I appreciate your concern for Angie's emotional state, Dr. Conrad—" especially when Angie's desires fell in so neatly with his own best interest "—and if she was cut anywhere but her face, I'd let you go ahead. But I learned a little from one of my son's playground injuries. The attending physician in the ER at the time advised me to wait for someone familiar with microsurgery to close it up. I've always been grateful for the advice. Without a doctor who has that type of experience, his scar, which right now you can barely see, would be much more noticeable. We'll do this my way," Lenore finished firmly.

Lenore braced for the rebuttal, and then, miraculously, Paul was there. If she'd learned anything on their trip, it was that Paul was good at being in charge. She'd let him take over the argument with the arrogant doctor.

"Paul!" she cried out as he strode over to them. "Am I ever glad to see you."

Paul's brow rose in evident surprise at her effusive greeting, but the truth was, she *was* happy to see him, and not just so he could do the insisting that a real doctor see Angie. She'd missed him. *Him.*

"Thank you for coming," he said by way of greeting.

It was then Lenore knew for sure she would have her work cut out for her if she wanted to straighten things out with him. Paul's greeting sounded very formal and stiff.

"I apologize for your being bothered. I won't forget my beeper again. I want to let Angie know I'm here, then I'll be right back so you can fill me in on what's going on, if you don't mind waiting to leave until then."

"Uh, no, of course not." Brrr. She felt a definite chill in the air. But then he gave her shoulder a brief squeeze before he went in to Angie. Was there hope?

Lenore waited outside the cubicle to allow Paul some time alone with his daughter. She refused to admit even to herself how disappointed she was that he hadn't seemed more pleased to see her, hadn't kissed her hello. There'd even been a generic, distracted quality about the shoulder squeeze, although it had been better than nothing.

"Well, of course he's distracted," she told herself. "He's concentrating on Angie and rightly so." Well, once they were done here, they'd go someplace and talk. She'd see to it. Maybe tonight. Surely they could get things sorted out? Lenore had missed Paul too badly the past few weeks not to try.

The vacation, Lenore told herself, had been time out of time, place out of place. They'd both been off-balance, and as a result, their relationship had been built on a shaky foundation. Hardly surprising. And most unfair to make any kind of judgment on the future of a relationship based on such out-of-the-ordinary circumstances.

Now that they were back in their real lives, Lenore assured herself, they'd be able to figure out the dynamics of this thing. She hoped.

"Okay, Lenore, tell me what's happening here."

Lenore jumped, jolted from her musings by Paul's low voice rumbling in her ear. "Paul! I thought you were still in with Angie."

"They've taken her for X rays, so I thought I'd better talk to you real fast. That is one unhappy little girl. All she wants to do is get out of here. Given her druthers, she'd opt for a bandage and forget the stitches the doctor says she needs."

"Of course. I'm sure the idea of somebody coming at her face with a needle and thread has got to be frightening."

"My gut instinct tells me she'll do much better once we get her home, into familiar surroundings."

"I agree." Angie was worn-out from everything she'd been through that day. One good look at her own bed and the poor kid would probably zonk right out.

"The quickest, most expedient way to achieve that would be to let this Dr. Conrad suture her. He says it'll only take four or five stitches."

Uh-oh. Why did she get the feeling Paul was about to—for the eight hundredth time—overrule her? Had all that thinking and stewing, all that analyzing of their relationship been way off base? Had her initial impression been the correct one after all? Lenore's heart sank. No matter how attached she'd become to Angie, how much she'd missed Paul, how much her body craved his, Lenore knew she couldn't tolerate marriage in a dictatorship. She just couldn't. "Letting Howser do the sewing would be the quickest way to get Angie home," Lenore cautiously agreed.

"I thought his name was Conrad."

"It was a joke. He reminds me of the kid on that old television show, 'Doogie Howser M.D.'"

Paul felt as if he were walking on eggshells. He wasn't a stupid man. He knew more than the health of young Dr. Conrad's ego hung on what happened here. Lenore was waiting to see on whose side he came down.

At first, when Lenore had told him to take the proverbial hike, he'd felt insulted, maligned and misunderstood. Every decision he'd made had been judicious and well thought out. It was hardly his fault Lenore had consistently been in the wrong. His way, at least, they'd had a vacation, and she should have been more appreciative. So yes, certainly he'd been upset, but he'd also felt a great deal of relief. He'd been getting sucked into a relationship that had deepened even while he'd helplessly watched. Paul hadn't been at all sure he was ready to deal with that kind of emotional commitment again, yet was unable to resist taking the plunge. He'd been grateful for the cooling-off period she'd suggested.

But then, as the days had passed without her, he'd realized that, ready or not, he was committed. Life had been hellish the past few weeks without Lenore. The men on his construction crew were all threatening to jump shop and leave him to his bad temper. Even Barb, whom he barely ever saw anyway, had suggested that he might want to consider staying out of the office more frequently. His own office, for God's sake.

Just looking at Lenore now, though, underlined the fact that, as far as his heart was concerned, the damage was done. He was in love with Lenore and wanted her for himself. Wanting and getting, however, were two different things.

Paul knew the only real value in a mistake was in what one learned from it. Lenore's response to their wonderful vacation together had taught him—big time. If he wanted to win her back, he'd damn well better listen to what she was saying. Unfortunately, what she was saying was in direct opposition to what his daughter—and therefore he—wanted to hear. He was caught between his own flesh and blood and the woman he loved. God, what a mess. Not exactly a rock and a hard place, but close enough.

He felt his way cautiously. "So we agree on that. Fine. Then why is the good doctor telling me you're dragging your pretty little heels?"

"He put it that way?"

"Not exactly. I'm not sure he appreciates your charms quite the way I do."

"Oh. Well, I don't appreciate his, either, so we're even. Just don't let him touch Angie's face."

"Why not?" Paul asked in what he hoped was a reasonable tone of voice, although reason, he somehow doubted, would never rank very highly in this relationship of theirs. He and Lenore struck something far more primitive in each other for something as insipid as *reasonableness* to come into much play.

"It's her face, Paul. She's a little girl and it's her *face!*"

"I've got a scar on my forehead. My mother said it made me look more interesting."

He had a point there. He was the most interesting man she'd ever known, bar none. She shook her head. "You're not a girl. Whatever happens here today, she'll have to live with it every time she looks in the mirror for the rest of her life."

"Angie doesn't seem to care about that," Paul countered. "She just wants out of here."

"Of course. She's too young and too upset to understand the whys and wherefores of what you'd be doing. But later on, when she's in her teens, she'll thank you."

That's what Paul had assumed about Lenore and some of the decisions he'd made on the camping trip. Would he ever understand women?

"I'm supposed to go in there and tell that sobbing child she can't go home, probably for several more hours, because even though there's a guy right here who says he can do the job and she knows it and wants him to do it so she can leave, we've decided in our infinite parental wisdom that we want somebody else?"

Lenore nodded her head firmly. "Yes." Please. For Angie and their relationship both.

Paul's sigh was deep and heartfelt. He was torn between the two people he loved most in this world. "It doesn't make sense. Conrad says he can do it."

It was Lenore's turn to sigh. Would she ever get through to him? So maybe on the trip, she'd been a little balky and needed a little push, but she was right on this one, there was no doubt in her mind. Would he listen? She prayed so. This was not in the same league as simply being afraid to try something new. In Lenore's estimation, it was quite possible Angie could come to resent her father greatly in years to come if this matter wasn't handled correctly. She loved him—them—and so she would continue to argue until she was blue in the face. Maybe she'd come to recognize her love too late to salvage things with Paul, but she couldn't leave him to make a mistake that would damage his relationship with his own child. Her relationship with him might be dead in the water, but theirs wasn't. Not yet. It would be her final act of love.

Lenore put her hands on Paul's shoulders and looked up pleadingly into his eyes. "Paul, listen to me. Conrad's a young intern who's all filled with himself because he made it through med school. He hasn't specialized yet and is just rotating through the ER. If the cut was anywhere else on Angie's body, I'd say fine, let him get the experience. But it's her face. If he does the work, she'll be more than likely left with a much bigger scar than necessary. And she'll have it for the rest of her life."

He was still not convinced. "She doesn't seem to care about that."

"Maybe not right now. But later she will. I guarantee it. You've been a father, a fabulous one, for seven years now. You know not all a parent's decisions are easy ones. She'll not only forgive you, she'll thank you."

Paul looked at her, then at the anxiously hovering Dr. Conrad. "He's going to be upset. And embarrassed."

Lenore shrugged. "I'm sorry about that, but my first concern, *our* first concern has to be what's best for Angela."

She watched him anxiously, having given her best arguments. They'd been good ones, too. If he worried more about upsetting the young doctor and Angie's tears than what was best in the long run for his daughter, she knew he was not the man for her. Would he listen?

Long moments passed. Hospital people bustled all around them, but Paul and Lenore were caught and held motionless in their own private time warp as they studied each other's eyes.

This was it. What would he decide?

Suddenly, Paul leaned down and kissed her. "All right, Lenore," he said. "We'll do this your way. I'll go tell Conrad to get a board-certified facial plastic surgeon in here. Maybe if we stop and pick up ice-cream cones on the way home, Angie'll forgive us."

"Maybe." Lenore smiled happily, knowing far more than the question of who would put in Angie's stitches had just been decided. Paul had acknowledged that she was his equal, that he would listen to her during those times when a decision had to be made. "We'll have to pick up Timmy at my neighbors'."

Paul looked surprised. "Of course. We'll rent a movie for the two of them to watch while Angie rests on the sofa tonight. You and I can talk. We have a lot to decide."

"Such as?" Lenore inquired saucily.

Paul kissed her, right there in the crowded emergency room, but it was more of a promise of the passion to come than anything else. "Such as the best way to combine two households into one."

"We could sell your house and you could move into mine," Lenore suggested.

"Your ceilings are too low and mine's got the company's offices already set up and running in it. We'll sell yours."

"We'll discuss it tonight," she said, knowing they would reach an equitable solution somehow now that they were really listening to each other.

"Count on it. You can also count on a very brief engagement," Paul informed her. "I'm the one having nightmares lately, and I need you in my bed to chase them away.'' He kissed her once again.

Lenore melted inside. She would never let this man go again.

"But first," Paul continued after reluctantly ending the kiss, "I've got to let Dr. Conrad know he's out of the running. I'll be right back. Don't go anywhere. I love you."

"I won't," Lenore promised. "I love you, too." And she went back in to wait for him with their daughter.

*   *   *   *   *

HE'S NOT JUST A MAN,
HE'S ONE OF OUR

FATHER BY MARRIAGE
Suzanne Carey

Investigator Jake McKenzie knew there was more to widowed mom
Holly Yarborough than met the eye. And he was right—she and
her little girl were *hiding* on her ranch. Jake had a job to do, but
how could he be Mr. Scrooge when this family was all he wanted
for Christmas?

Fall in love with our Fabulous Fathers!

Coming in December, only from

Silhouette
R O M A N C E™

MILLION DOLLAR SWEEPSTAKES (III)

No purchase necessary. To enter, follow the directions published. Method of entry may vary. For eligibility, entries must be received no later than March 31, 1996. No liability is assumed for printing errors, lost, late or misdirected entries. Odds of winning are determined by the number of eligible entries distributed and received. Prizewinners will be determined no later than June 30, 1996.

Sweepstakes open to residents of the U.S. (except Puerto Rico), Canada, Europe and Taiwan who are 18 years of age or older. All applicable laws and regulations apply. Sweepstakes offer void wherever prohibited by law. Values of all prizes are in U.S. currency. This sweepstakes is presented by Torstar Corp., its subsidiaries and affiliates, in conjunction with book, merchandise and/or product offerings. For a copy of the Official Rules send a self-addressed, stamped envelope (WA residents need not affix return postage) to: MILLION DOLLAR SWEEPSTAKES (III) Rules, P.O. Box 4573, Blair, NE 68009, USA.

EXTRA BONUS PRIZE DRAWING

No purchase necessary. The Extra Bonus Prize will be awarded in a random drawing to be conducted no later than 5/30/96 from among all entries received. To qualify, entries must be received by 3/31/96 and comply with published directions. Drawing open to residents of the U.S. (except Puerto Rico), Canada, Europe and Taiwan who are 18 years of age or older. All applicable laws and regulations apply; offer void wherever prohibited by law. Odds of winning are dependent upon number of eligibile entries received. Prize is valued in U.S. currency. The offer is presented by Torstar Corp., its subsidiaries and affiliates in conjunction with book, merchandise and/or product offering. For a copy of the Official Rules governing this sweepstakes, send a self-addressed, stamped envelope (WA residents need not affix return postage) to: Extra Bonus Prize Drawing Rules, P.O. Box 4590, Blair, NE 68009, USA.

SWP-S1195

HAPPY HOLIDAYS!

Silhouette Romance celebrates the holidays with
six heartwarming stories of the greatest gift of all—
love that lasts a lifetime!

#1120 *Father by Marriage*
by Suzanne Carey

#1121 *The Merry Matchmakers*
by Helen R. Myers

#1122 *It Must Have Been the Mistletoe*
by Moyra Tarling

#1123 *Jingle Bell Bride*
by Kate Thomas

#1124 *Cody's Christmas Wish*
by Sally Carleen

#1125 *The Cowboy and the Christmas Tree*
by DeAnna Talcott

COMING IN DECEMBER FROM

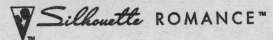

COMING NEXT MONTH

You're About to Become a *Privileged Woman*

Reap the rewards of fabulous free gifts and benefits with proofs-of-purchase from Silhouette and Harlequin books

Pages & Privileges™

It's our way of thanking you for buying our books at your favorite retail stores.

PROOF OF PURCHASE
SR-PP70
Offer expires October 31, 1996

**Harlequin and Silhouette—
the most privileged readers in the world!**

For more information about Harlequin and Silhouette's PAGES & PRIVILEGES program call the Pages & Privileges Benefits Desk: 1-503-794-2499

Silhouette®

SR-PP70